Witch Is Why A Pin Dropped

Published by Implode Publishing Ltd
© Implode Publishing Ltd 2017

Chapter 1

"I told you that Mum would like the condiment set," Jack said.

"You did say that."

"You just can't bring yourself to admit that you were wrong about it, can you? Didn't you see her put them in the cupboard with all of the other things she keeps for special occasions?"

"I did see that."

"Come on, Jill. Why don't you just say what's on your mind?"

"I'm sure you're right, and that your mother keeps all her favourite things in that cupboard. Or—" I hesitated.

"Yes? Go on. Spit it out."

"Or maybe it's where she puts all the stuff she never wants to lay eyes on again. Just saying."

"That's because you don't know 'class' when you see it."

"You're right. What was I thinking? A golden parrots condiment set? Pure class."

It was Monday morning, and I'd somehow survived the weekend's golden wedding anniversary party. Jack was pondering which awful cereal to have for breakfast. Meanwhile, my sausage cob was going down a treat.

"I thought the party went really well," he said.

"Except for the part where your mother hates me."

"Mum doesn't hate you. Why would you think that?"

"She practically ignored me all the time we were there. She spent more time talking to Grandma than she did to me."

"You're imagining things. Dad definitely likes you."

"Your dad is really sweet."

"Your grandmother certainly likes her drink. What I don't understand is why she thought my parents were teetotal."

"Grandma can get confused sometimes. By the way, did you hear your parents say how much they liked her present?"

"I don't recall."

"Yes, you do. They were thrilled with the one-year's subscription to Netflix."

"The twins seemed to enjoy themselves, but what's up with their dancing? It looked like they were having some kind of seizure."

"It is pretty tragic." I laughed.

"Your grandmother certainly has the moves. Did you see her dancing with Dad?"

"I could hardly miss them."

Despite Jack's reassurances, I felt like his mother had taken against me for some reason. When we'd first arrived at their house, his father had given me a big bear hug, and greeted me like a long lost relative. By contrast, his mother had shaken my hand. After the initial small talk, I'd barely spoken to her again. Maybe it was just my paranoia, but every time I went near her, she seemed to find some excuse to move away. Perhaps she was upset because it had taken so long for me to get around to visiting them? Whatever the reason, I wasn't in any hurry to repeat the experience.

After Jack had left for work, I decided I needed a

custard cream or three.

What? The sausage cob had been exceptionally small, so obviously I was still peckish.

Horror of horrors—custard creams were there none. How could that possibly be? I'd bought three packets only two days earlier. Who could have eaten them all? It must have been Jack.

I could have ignored the craving, and gone to work, but why should I? I deserved a custard cream after the ordeal of the anniversary party.

At first, I didn't think there was anyone behind the counter in the corner shop, but then I caught sight of the top of Little Jack Corner's head.

"Hi." I leaned over the counter.

"Good morning." He stepped up onto the box that he kept behind there. "I didn't hear you come in. Custard creams, I assume?"

"That's right." Should I have been worried that he knew me so well? "I'll take four packets, please."

"You get through a lot of these."

"They're mainly for Jack, my partner. I just eat the occasional one."

"Will there be anything else this morning? I'm running a special offer on tofu."

"Tempting as that is, I'm okay, thanks."

"Before you go, you'll want to hear today's thought for the day."

I very much doubted that.

"He who laughs last, laughs last."

"Shouldn't that be 'longest'?"

"Longest what?"

"Never mind. Thanks for that."

Back at the house, I washed down two custard creams with a nice cup of tea. I was ready for anything the world had to throw at me.

"Jill! Do you have a minute?" Megan Lovemore, my next-door neighbour had obviously been waiting for me to leave for work.

"Sure. How are things?"

"Okay, thanks. The gardening business is booming. I'm hoping to give up the modelling within the next few months."

"And your new boyfriend?"

"Ryan's lovely. I wasn't sure about him at first, but now, it's like we were made for one another."

"That's great."

"This might sound like a strange question, Jill, but do you know much about teeth?"

"Why? Do you have a toothache?"

"No. It's not for me. It's—err—well—it's a bit awkward."

"Go on."

"It's Ryan. I've noticed that he has two really big teeth. I suppose they must be wisdom teeth or something."

Oh bum!

"Are they causing him problems?"

"No. He hasn't mentioned them, but I have to be honest, they kind of freak me out a bit. The really weird part is that they don't seem to be there all the time."

"What do you mean?"

"I know that sounds crazy, but it's like sometimes they're there, and sometimes they're not."

"Have you said anything to him?"

"No. I don't want to upset or embarrass him. I just wondered if you'd ever come across anything like that?"

"I can't say I have."

"Oh well." She sighed. "I suppose I'll get used to them. He is a great guy."

Poor Megan. She'd be even more freaked out if she knew that her boyfriend was a bloodsucking vampire.

**

The bottle tops were back on the toll booth windows; that could mean only one thing—Mr Ivers must be in residence.

"Jill. I'm glad I caught you."

That made one of us, then.

"Can it wait? I'm running a little late for work this morning, Mr Ivers."

"I have good news and bad news."

If I was lucky, the good news would be that he was emigrating to Australia.

"The bad news first. I'm afraid I won't be producing any more movie newsletters."

How was that bad news? "Really? That is a shame."

"The good news is that I've just published the first copy of Toppers News."

"For bottle top enthusiasts, I assume."

"Indeed. The toppers community is in desperate need of good quality journalistic coverage of the industry. That's where I come in. And, as promised, I'm offering a special discount to my movie newsletter subscribers. Fifty per cent off the normal subscription price."

"That's a very generous offer, but I have to decline. I really have no interest in bottle tops."

"Are you sure? The offer is only good for one month."

"I'm positive. To be honest, I find it hard to imagine that many people will take up the offer. It's quite a leap from movies to bottle tops."

"You may be right about that, but it's of no real concern. I've just signed an agreement with the proprietor of Top Of The World."

"Norman?"

"You know him?"

"Norman and I go way back."

"He has agreed to sell my new publication in his shop, and from all accounts, it's already selling like hotcakes."

"That's great. Anyway, here's the toll fee. I have to get going."

Result! I'd managed to get rid of the stupid movie newsletter at long last.

***

I was desperate for a coffee, so I called into Coffee Triangle on my way to work.

"Would you like a tambourine with your latte, madam?"

"Why not?" It was ages since I'd shaken one. There was something curiously therapeutic about it, which was more than could be said for the sinister triangle.

"Can I interest you in one of our new loyalty cards?"

"I suppose so."

My purse was already bursting at the seams with them. It seemed like there was a loyalty card for everything these days. I even had one from the chiropodist following my problem with an in-grown toenail. Still, I was something of a regular in Coffee Triangle, so I might as well reap the benefits.

The loyalty card was shaped like a triangle, which gave me the creeps a little. Printed on it, was a number of small images—one for each of the different percussion instruments.

"Does it work the same way as usual? Do you mark off one of the images each time I buy a coffee?"

"Not quite. We wanted to do something a little different. The way it works is that you can only cross out an image if you come in on the day related to that image. For example, if you buy a coffee on drum day, you get to cross off the drum."

"If I understand you correctly, in order to earn a free coffee, I would have to come in on the day for each of the different instruments? Including drum and gong?"

"Precisely."

How very cunning.

***

I'd more or less got used to the idea of having two PAs. I'm sure some of my visitors still found it a little unusual, but no one had complained so far. Mrs V and Jules had got over the initial friction, and the new arrangement now seemed to be working just fine.

Whoops! Spoke too soon.

The two desks were usually side by side, but now there was a filing cabinet between them. It appeared to be acting as some kind of makeshift screen.

"Please tell me you two haven't fallen out again."

"We haven't," Jules said.

"What's with the filing cabinet?"

"It's the Washbridge Annual Knitting competition." Mrs V looked up from her knitting. "We're both going to enter, but I don't want Jules to copy me."

"Dream on." Jules scoffed. "You're more likely to copy me."

"The day I need to copy you, young lady, is the day I hang up my knitting needles."

"Better hang them up now, then."

Thank goodness there was no friction between them. "How long is this new arrangement likely to last?"

"It won't take *me* long," Jules said. "But it might take Annabel some time just to come up with an idea."

"You talk a good game, Missy." Mrs V put down her knitting. "How about you put your money where your mouth is?"

"What did you have in mind?" Jules stood up.

"A small wager. Whichever one of us places highest in the overall competition is the winner."

"You're on. You can't get any higher than first place, and that's where I'll come."

"We'll see about that. Shall we say ten pounds?"

"Make it twenty."

"Okay." Mrs V turned to me. "Jill can hold the money."

This wasn't going to turn out well. Whichever one of them lost would not be a happy bunny.

***

When I walked into my office, Winky had his back to

me; he appeared to be talking to himself.

"I'm not stupid, Winky. You can't fool me with your ghost cat trick again. I know Lenny isn't here, so you're not getting double helpings of salmon."

"I'm not talking to Lenny. If you must know, I'm talking to my friend, Bob." He pointed at the floor.

"There isn't anyone there."

"Yes there is. Look."

I walked over, and crouched down to get a better view. At first, I didn't see anything, but then I noticed something small and black.

"The spider?"

"Yes. That's Bob."

"You're having a conversation with a spider?" I laughed.

"Go ahead. Make fun of me, but Bob is the only friend I have. You don't know what it's like to be left in here all alone for hours on end. If it wasn't for Bob, I don't know what I'd do."

Now I just felt bad.

Chapter 2

"What's going on out there?" Kathy had dropped by the office on her day off. "Why are Mrs V and Jules both in today?"

"It's been going on for a while. Mrs V couldn't stand the idea of staying at home, so she's decided to come in on her days off."

"Did you have to buy another desk?"

"No. Armi came up with one."

"Speaking of the Armitage clan, have you had any more problems with Gordon Armitage?"

"No, but I'm sure I will."

"Pete and I really enjoyed the anniversary party."

"I'm glad someone did. Jack's mother hates me."

"What makes you say that? She seemed really nice to me. And his dad."

"Jack's dad is a sweetie, but his mother did her best to avoid me all day."

"You're being paranoid."

"I'm not. I reckon it's because it took us so long to get around to visiting her."

"I can think of one sure-fire way to win her over."

"Oh?"

"Give her a grandchild."

"I'm not having a baby just to get on the right side of Jack's mother."

"It's time you and Jack were thinking about it."

"Thanks for the input. Now, was there some particular reason you came over?"

"Actually, I need a favour."

"How very unusual."

"You make it sound like I'm always asking for favours."

"That sounds about right. What is it this time?"

"There's a travelling funfair on Washbridge Green, this week. I promised I'd take the kids, but Pete has to work late every day on the Washbridge House contract. I thought you might like to come with us."

"To a funfair?"

"Yeah. You might enjoy it."

"From my experience of them, they are neither *fun* nor *fair*. And besides, it'll be muddy."

"Please, Jill. If you won't do it for me, do it for your nephew and niece. We'll only be there an hour. Two, tops."

"Are you using the kids to guilt-trip me?"

"Of course I am."

"Go on, then. I suppose so."

"Thanks. Oh, by the way, your grandmother said I should remind you about the 'tax'. She said you'd know what she meant."

"Right."

Grandma had been on my case for a few days about the upcoming meeting of the Combined Sup Council. She was relying on me to block the proposal to tax sups who lived in the human world. I had no idea how she expected me to influence the vote, but I knew one thing for sure—I'd be in big trouble if I didn't manage it.

"Your grandmother seemed to enjoy the anniversary party. So much for your teetotal ruse."

"I couldn't believe it when she showed up. She's like a bad penny."

"Is Jack looking forward to the 'We' concert?"

"You mean the one that everyone is going to—except

for poor little me? The one where I have to stay at home all by myself?"

"Don't give me that. It might work on Jack, but it doesn't cut any ice with me. I know you don't want to go."

**

Things were pretty quiet, work-wise, so after Kathy had gone on her way, I magicked myself over to Aunt Lucy's house. I knew I could rely on her for a cup of tea and a slice of cake.

"Look at this stupid thing." She handed me an envelope.

"Dinner and dance? I thought you liked to go dancing?"

"I do normally, but who in their right mind would want to go to the Grim Reaper Annual Dinner and Dance? Those people are seriously weird."

"They're Lester's work colleagues."

"I don't need reminding of that. I was hoping he would have grown tired of that awful job by now, but if anything, he's even more enthusiastic."

"You really will have to get over this, Aunt Lucy."

"That's easier said than done. How would you feel if Jack came home every night, and talked about how many people he'd 'despatched' that day?"

"Point taken. Won't you be going to the dance, then?"

"I don't know—probably not. Lester says he's going with or without me."

"Hmm? And you're okay with that?"

"What do you mean?"

"I imagine there'll be lots of attractive female reapers

there. But, I'm sure there's no need to worry."

"I hadn't thought about that. I suppose I could make the effort. Like you said, I do enjoy a good dance. Would you come shopping with me, and help me to pick out a new dress?"

"Of course."

***

After leaving Aunt Lucy's, I decided to pay a visit to Cuppy C for coffee and a blueberry muffin.

What? I know I'd only just had a slice of cake, but I burned those calories off on the walk over. Who are you calling delusional?

Huh? What on earth was going on? There was no sign of Amber or Pearl. Instead, Alan and William were behind the tea room counter.

"Guys?"

"Hi, Jill." Alan greeted me with a toothy smile, which reminded me that there was something I needed to ask his advice on.

"What can I get for you, Jill?" William said.

"First of all, you'd better tell me what's going on in here. Are the twins poorly?"

"No. They're both fine. In fact, they've gone shopping."

"I didn't realise that you two ever worked in here."

"This is our first time," Alan turned to William. "Do you want to tell her, or shall I?"

"You go ahead."

"Okay. Why don't we grab a table, Jill? William can bring over your drink and your muffin."

"How did you know that's what I wanted?"

"Everyone knows about your blueberry muffin addiction."

Alan and I took a window seat.

"Go on, then," I prompted. "Tell me why you two are in here. I'm intrigued."

"The four of us had a night out recently. I can't remember exactly what was said, but the twins got upset. They thought William and I were insinuating that they had it easy, working here in Cuppy C. We weren't really having a go at them—it was just a bit of a laugh."

By then, William had joined us, and he picked up the story, "The girls said we wouldn't be able to take the pace of working in the shop. We weren't going to let that go, so we offered to prove we could do it. Before we knew it, we'd arranged to spend some time working here."

"Are you just here for the day?"

"No. We agreed to work here for three days. The twins are convinced we won't make it past day one."

"How's it going so far?"

"I'm actually enjoying it," William said.

"Me too." Alan nodded. "I thought I'd hate every moment, but the customers are really nice, and it's not that difficult, despite what the twins would have you believe."

As I took a sip of my tea, I noticed something through the window. "What's going on across the road?"

"You mean with Best Cakes?" Alan followed my gaze.

"Yeah. The shop looks as if it's closed."

"It's been closed for a couple of days."

"Any idea why?"

"Not a clue."

"How very strange. Anyway, on a totally unrelated

matter, can I pick your brain, Alan?"

"Good luck with that." William laughed.

"Take no notice of him," Alan said. "How can I help?"

"I have a friend in the human world who is dating a vampire. She's a little freaked out by his fangs, although thankfully, she thinks they're just weird wisdom teeth. It seems that he's oblivious to the fact that they are showing."

"He needs StopFangs."

"What's that?"

If he rubs it on his gums where his fangs would normally appear, it will solve the problem."

"How does it work?"

"I don't know the ins-and-outs, but it basically stops the fangs appearing for about twelve hours."

"That sounds ideal. Would you jot down the name of the product for me, so I don't forget it?"

The guys were back at work behind the counter; they were naturals. William was a real whizz with the coffee machine—much better than I'd been when I'd tried my hand at it. And they both seemed to have a great rapport with the customers.

***

After I'd magicked myself back to the office, I spent a couple of hours just tinkering around, and then I called it a day. What I really needed was a juicy case to get my teeth into, but there was precious little sign of that happening.

Mrs V and Jules were both still hard at it—knitting

needles a go-go. Jules was chuntering to herself as she knitted.

"Having problems, Jules?"

"It's not the knitting." She looked up. "It's Gilbert. He just rang and asked me to run an errand for him. He wants me to go into that creepy bottle top shop."

Never had a description been more apt.

"Does he want you to buy some bottle tops for him?"

"No, thank goodness. He's heard there's a newsletter called Toppers News. He wants me to buy him a copy before they're all sold out. I just hope that no one I know sees me go in there. I don't want anyone thinking I'm a sad sack."

"As it happens, I know the guy who writes Toppers News."

"Is he a friend of yours?"

"I wouldn't go that far."

***

On my drive home, I was listening to the radio. Lee Sparks was the DJ on Radio Wash's drivetime slot. Although he played the usual mix of 'blah' music, the guy could be quite entertaining at times. I'd heard a lot of people say that they found Sparks' humour to be puerile, but he made me laugh.

What did that say about me? Don't answer that—don't you know a rhetorical question when you see one?

"All of you out there in Wash Land, if you enjoyed that tune, honk your horn."

He'd no sooner said the words than I heard a number of car horns sound around me.

"Listeners, we have a visitor in the studio. Jay, would you like to say hello to the Washbridge public?"

That was followed by a few seconds of silence, as though he'd turned off his microphone. Then he was back again, but his voice had changed. He sounded scared.

"No! Please! Don't! Aaarghh!"

What was that all about? You could never be sure with Lee Sparks. He loved doing wind-ups live on air. If I was hoping for some kind of explanation, I was to be disappointed because what followed was several minutes of dead air, until eventually the music started up again.

As I got out of my car, I happened to glance at next-door's front window. What I saw shocked me. Clare, our new neighbour, was standing in the lounge, and she appeared to be wearing a traditional witch's outfit. I was stunned—and even more stunned when Tony, her husband, appeared next to her. He was dressed in a traditional wizard's outfit. I knew they weren't sups, so why were they dressed like that? I hurried into the house before they spotted me.

Under Jack's egalitarian system, it was my turn to make dinner, so I ordered in pizza.

What? Of course that still counts.

"We should probably go around next door to introduce ourselves," Jack said.

"I've already met them."

"I haven't. We could take them a bottle of wine as a 'welcome to the neighbourhood' gift."

"I'm not sure that's a good idea. I think they might be a couple of weirdos."

"Why would you say that?"

"When I came home tonight, I saw them standing in their lounge. They were wearing weird costumes."

"What kind of weird costumes?"

"She was dressed as a witch. He was dressed as a wizard."

"Are you sure about that? You have been known to jump to the wrong conclusion."

"That's not true."

"What about the time you thought Mr Kilbride was into the occult?"

"That was a simple mistake; I couldn't understand his accent. Anyway, I saw these two with my own eyes. There's something decidedly weird going on next door."

Just then, Jack's phone rang.

"Mum? Yes, we had a great time. Jill? Yes, she said it was great to meet you both at long last. How is Dad?"

"What did she want?" I asked when Jack finished on the call.

"Nothing much. She was just checking that we'd enjoyed the party."

"What did she say about me?"

"Just that it was nice to meet you at last."

A likely story.

Chapter 3

I hadn't had a chance to look through Imelda Barrowtop's journal since before the anniversary party. It wasn't something I could do when anyone else was around; that's why I was up at five in the morning. I figured that would give me at least an hour and a half to study it before Jack got up.

I'd been shocked when I'd found the entry referring to the red haired, red bearded man, but having had more time to reflect on it, I'd come to the conclusion that it was no more than a coincidence. There were lots of men with red hair and red beards, and there probably always had been. The fact that they'd had the same name definitely made it a little weird, but it was nothing to get freaked out about.

I made coffee, and settled down in the lounge. There were hundreds of pages in the journal. For the most part, the entries were all very run-of-the-mill. It seemed that Magna Mondale would meet up with Imelda Barrowtop periodically. When they met, Imelda would make a record of everything that Magna told her. The whole thing seemed nonsensical to me. Why bother?

I was just about to give up on it when I came across an entry which I read, and then re-read.

Magna was more upset than I've ever seen her before. She found the red haired, red bearded man dead on her doorstep. He had a pendant in his hands with the initials 'JB' engraved on it. Magna is going out of her mind with worry.

I threw the journal onto the sofa. What on earth was going on? Was this some kind of elaborate hoax? What other explanation could there be? I'd discovered the body of a red haired, red bearded man, close to my office. Not long after that, Mrs V had found a black box in the linen basket; it had contained a pendant with the same two initials engraved on it: *JB*. I still had it, hidden in a drawer upstairs.

I'd been reading for some time without finding anything of any significance, and then I came to this chilling entry:

Magna seems really scared, but she won't say why. She has sealed her spell book in the basement of her house, and has cast a spell that will prevent anyone gaining entry. Apparently, she has also left a message inside the room, but she wouldn't tell me what it was, or who it was for. I'm really worried about her.

That was the last entry except for a single line of text on the following page:

Magna is dead.

"Jill! What are you doing up at this unearthly hour? Are you okay?"

I hadn't heard Jack come downstairs.

"I couldn't sleep."

"What's that you're reading?"

"It's nothing. Just something from a case I'm working on." I grabbed the journal, and hurried upstairs before he could ask any awkward questions. "Make me another cup of coffee would you, sweetness?"

Over breakfast, Jack had his nose stuck to his phone.

"Whatever happened to the art of conversation?" I said.

"Sorry. I was just looking at the local news. One of the DJs at Radio Wash was murdered yesterday, while he was broadcasting his show."

"What?" I snatched the phone from him. "Let me see."

"Hey. Do you mind?"

"It's Lee Sparks. I was listening to his drivetime show when it happened. He said something about someone coming into the studio, and then seemed to get a little panicked. I didn't think much of it at the time because I assumed it was some kind of prank. He was always messing around like that."

I handed back the phone.

"It looks like Leo Riley is going to be busy." Jack grinned.

***

For once, Jack and I left for work at the same time. As we did, our new neighbours came out of their house.

"I should go over and introduce myself," Jack said.

"Wait!" I grabbed his arm, and said in a hushed voice. "Be careful."

"What are you talking about?"

"Don't you remember what I told you about them being dressed in weird costumes?"

"Hi!" Tony called. He and Clare had spotted us, and were on their way over.

"Oh, hi." I smiled. "I didn't see you there."

"Hi, I'm Jack Maxwell."

"I'm Tony and this is Clare, my wife."

"Nice to meet you, Jack," said Clare, the pseudo-witch.

"How are you settling in?" Jack asked.

"We love it." She gushed. "Don't we, Tony?"

"So far, so good."

"Did you enjoy your party?" I said.

"Sorry?" Fake wizard, Tony, pretended to be puzzled.

"Last night when I got home, I saw you through the window. You were dressed as a witch and a wizard. Was it a fancy dress party?"

Jack forced a nervous laugh. "It's none of our business, Jill."

"That's okay." Tony looked around to see if anyone else was in earshot. "Actually, you've discovered our deep, dark secret."

Clare giggled, and for a horrible moment, I thought they were going to give us the down and dirty on their sex life. "We share a passion for cosplay. In fact, that's how we met."

"Cosplay?" Jack looked puzzled; he'd led such a sheltered life.

"It's where people dress up as their favourite comic book characters," I said.

"Not just comic books. TV, movie and game characters, too." Clare corrected me. "We go to lots of cosplay conventions. At least one a month. This weekend it's SupsCon. Have you heard of it?"

Neither of us had.

"It's a convention based around the supernatural world. We're going as Marcia and Zorta."

Jack's nonplussed expression no doubt mirrored my own.

"From the TV show, Marcia and Zorta," Tony said. "You must have seen it?"

"We don't watch much TV."

"You really should check it out," Clare chimed in. "It's brilliant. We were trying on our costumes last night when you saw us. I hope we didn't give you too much of a shock. Nobody wants to think they're living next door to a witch, do they?"

"That would be terrible." I smiled.

"You two should totally come with us." Clare turned to her husband. "There are still tickets available, aren't there?"

I needed to kill this stupid idea quickly. "Thanks, but it's not really our—"

"We'd love to." Jack jumped in.

Was he out of his freaking mind?

"Don't you remember, Jack?" I glared at him. "We have that *thing* this Saturday."

"What *thing*?"

"The *thing*—the one that we have on Saturday."

"No, Saturday is free. I'm sure."

"We could get you a couple of tickets." Tony offered.

"That would be great," Jack said. "I'll let you have the cash."

"Fantastic! You're going to love it. Anyway, we'd better get off or we'll be late for work."

"Why are you looking at me like that?" Jack asked, in all innocence, after they'd left.

"Cosplay? Really?"

"It sounds like fun."

"I suppose you think having a root canal sounds like fun, too?"

"What will we go as? We can't go as a witch and wizard because Tony and Clare are already doing that. You wouldn't make a very good witch, anyway."

"What do you mean?"

"You're too attractive. Witches are all ugly."

"Where did you read that? Wiki-witches? Are you really sure you want to go to this thing? There are much more exciting ways we could spend our Saturday."

"Such as?"

"I believe they're repainting the town hall. We could always go and watch it dry."

***

"Cosplay? Seriously?" I was still chuntering to myself after I'd arrived in Washbridge.

"Sorry?" The parking attendant gave me a puzzled look.

"I was just talking to myself. Ignore me."

As he went on his way, I could hear him muttering about the 'crazies' he had to put up with.

I was almost at the office when my phone rang. I was sure it would be Jack, wanting to tell me what costume he'd decided to wear.

"What now?" I barked.

"Oh, dear. Did I call at a bad time?"

"Sorry, Aunt Lucy. I didn't realise it was you. I'm having a bad morning."

"Nothing serious, I hope?"

"Jack has just signed us up to go to some stupid supernatural cosplay thing on Saturday."

"That sounds like fun. I love cosplay."

"You do?"

"Oh, yes. When I was younger, I went to loads of them. You should go as a witch. Just for the irony."

"According to Jack, I'd make a terrible witch. Apparently, I'm not ugly enough."

She laughed. "What will you go as, then?"

"Nothing, if I can help it. I'm still working on ways to get out of it. Anyway, you called me?"

"Yes, but seeing as you're already having a bad day, maybe I should leave it for another time?"

"No, it's okay. I'm only blowing off steam. What is it?"

"You're never going to believe this, but I had a phone call from Miles Best. He asked me to get in touch with you, to see if you'd be prepared to meet with him and Mindy."

"Did he say what it's about?"

"He didn't go into detail, but he did say that he needed your help."

"Hmm? I wouldn't trust that pair as far as I could throw them."

"I'm not a fan either, but he did sound pretty desperate."

"Okay. I guess it can't do any harm to hear him out. Did he give you his phone number?"

I gave Miles a call, and he did indeed sound in a bad way. He said he couldn't go into detail over the phone, and asked if I'd pay him a visit at Best Cakes.

"Is the shop open again now?"

"No. You'll need to go around to the back door."

"Okay. I'll pop over later."

***

Mrs V was by herself.

"Morning, Mrs V."

She was so engrossed in her knitting project that she

barely managed a grunt.

"The sky is very green today."

Another grunt.

"I thought I might do a little brain surgery on the cat this morning."

And that made a hat-trick of grunts.

As soon as I walked through the door to my office, Winky moved his paws behind his back, as though he was trying to hide something.

"What's that?"

"What's what?"

"Whatever it is you have behind your back."

"There's nothing behind my back." He showed me one paw, and then the other.

"It's still behind your back. You just moved it between your paws. Do you think I'm stupid?"

"Do you want the truth, or would you prefer me to be polite?"

"Neither, and you know what? I don't care what's behind your back. You can keep your little secret."

I was onto his game; he was trying to draw me in.

I'd been at my desk for about fifteen minutes when Mrs V came through.

"Client?" I said more out of hope than expectation.

"No, dear. I wanted to show you my competition entry. It's coming along nicely."

"Right." The excitement never ended.

"It's a tea cosy." She held it up.

"A what?"

"A tea cosy. Surely you've heard of a tea cosy?"

"It looks like a hat."

"No it doesn't!" She passed it to me. "See that hole? That's where the spout comes out."

"What spout?"

"You, young people. I suppose you've only ever made a cup of tea by putting a tea bag into a cup?"

"Is there another way?"

"There's the correct way, which is to brew the tea in a teapot. A tea cosy goes over the teapot to keep it —"

"Cosy?"

"Warm."

"I see. Will anyone else know what it is? Won't everyone just think it's a hat?"

"Thankfully, the judges are all intelligent people."

Burn!

"It's very colourful."

"I have the Chameleon Wool to thank for that. Now that it's working properly, it does make life so much easier." She took the tea cosy back from me. "What's the verdict? Do you think I'm in with a chance?"

"Without a doubt. It's bound to be the best tea cosy there."

Chapter 4

Best Cakes was still closed, and as far as I could tell, there was nothing to indicate when it was going to reopen.

I'd first encountered Miles Best at the twins' school reunion. They'd had a crush on him back in their schooldays, and had both been excited to meet him again. That hadn't worked out as they'd hoped because the years had not been kind to him. And, being the superficial pair they were, the twins had no interest in Miles mark two.

Ever since then, Miles and his partner, Mindy, had waged some kind of vendetta, not only against the twins, but also against me. They'd even tried to get one over on Grandma, but that had proven to be a big mistake. Given our history, I was rather surprised that he would want my help.

I would have to be on my guard.

"Jill, come on in." Miles greeted me at the rear door to the shop. "Thanks for agreeing to see us."

He and Mindy lived in a small apartment over the shop. Miles led the way upstairs and into the lounge, where Mindy was already seated on the sofa.

"Hi, Jill." She smiled.

"Hi."

"Would you like a drink?"

"No, thanks. I'd rather get straight down to business."

"You're probably wondering why the shop is closed?" Miles said.

"Yeah. I noticed it was shut when I was in Cuppy C, yesterday."

"The authorities closed us down because a number of

pins have been found in some of our cakes."

"Goodness. Was anyone hurt?"

"Fortunately, no, but I dread to think what might have happened if someone had actually swallowed one."

"Do you have any idea how the pins got into the cakes?"

"No. That's what we're hoping you'll find out."

"I have to say, Miles, I'm surprised you would ask *me* to investigate. Given our history, that is."

"I know, and I realise that most of that has been on our side."

"*Most?*" If he thought I was about to let him off the hook, he was mistaken.

"You're right. We've done some unforgivable things for which I'm truly sorry, but we really do need your help now. The authorities are going to allow us to re-open tomorrow, but they've made it clear that if there's any repetition, we'll be closed down permanently."

"I'm surprised they've given you another chance."

"They're only doing it because I managed to convince them that we'd traced the problem to one batch from a single supplier."

"And did you have it out with that supplier?"

"No, because that was a lie. We're absolutely certain that the problem isn't with our suppliers. The pins were put into the cakes after they arrived at the shop."

"It's those two girls!" Mindy spat the words. "Flora and Laura."

"We don't know that," Miles snapped. "We have three other part-time staff. It could be any one of them. Or even an outside party."

"It's those girls." Mindy turned to face me. "You know

what they're like, Jill. You saw them in action at Cuppy C."

It was true. The two ice maidens had done their best to sabotage the twins' business, but what Mindy had failed to mention was that they had done so at the bidding of Miles. Being the diplomat that I am, I decided not to mention that.

"What exactly do you want me to do? I can hardly work undercover in the shop because Flora and Laura both know me."

"You're the best P.I. in Washbridge. Everyone knows that," Miles said. "Plus, you're the most powerful witch in Candlefield. If anyone can get to the bottom of this, you can."

"How do I know I can trust you, Miles? It wouldn't be the first time you've tried to get one over on me."

"We're desperate, Jill. If we lose Best Cakes, we'll lose everything. We'll pay you twice your normal fee."

"If I agree to do this—and that's a very big 'if'—I won't want any payment."

The two of them exchanged a puzzled look.

"What I do want is your solemn promise that you'll never do anything else to hurt me, my family or our businesses."

"Agreed." Miles didn't hesitate. "You have our word, doesn't she, Mindy?"

"Yes, of course." Mindy nodded.

"I have one other condition."

"Name it."

"I must insist on being able to conduct this investigation in my own way. And that means I will tell no one, including either of you, how or when I'll do it."

"Agreed," Miles said. "But you need to catch whoever it is quickly—before they get us closed down for good."

"Okay. I'll take the case, but you'll need to warn Flora and Laura that I may pay a visit, and that I should be allowed to go anywhere in the shop."

"What shall I tell them you're doing?"

"You'll have to lie—you're good at that. Why not tell them that you're pretending to call a truce with me, so that you can get a look at Cuppy C in return? That sounds evil enough to be plausible."

***

It was possible that I'd just made one of the biggest mistakes of my life. I would definitely have to be on my guard; at the first sign of any skulduggery I would make Miles and Mindy wish they'd never been born.

I was just about to magic myself back to the office when I noticed that Cuppy C was incredibly busy. Alan and William had agreed to run the shop for three days. How would they cope with so many customers? I thought I'd better check in on them. If they were really struggling, I could always volunteer my services for an hour.

What do you mean that would do more harm than good? Cheek! When I want your opinion, I'll ask for it.

As it turned out, I needn't have worried. The shop was indeed much busier than usual, but the two guys seemed to be coping admirably. It was obvious that both of them were every bit as confident on the coffee machine as the twins. They made me look like a rank amateur. As I waited in-line to be served, it occurred to me that there was an unusually high number of young females in the shop. Normally, the customers were a mix of ages, and as many couples as singles. Not today. A quick scan of the shop revealed that at least seventy-five per cent of the customers were young females under thirty-five.

A pretty young witch joined the queue behind me.

"Are you here for the eye-candy, too?" She gestured towards Alan and William. "I don't usually come in here because those two ditsy girls get on my nerves, but then I found out that these two hunks were working here."

"How did you hear?"

"I got a text from my friend, Polly. She was in here yesterday."

That explained the sudden popularity of the tea room, and the marked change in the demographic of the customers. They were all here to see Alan and William. Oh dear. That wouldn't go down well with Amber and Pearl.

Snigger.

***

Why, oh why, had I let myself be talked into going to the funfair?

"Auntie Jill!" Lizzie came charging over, and threw herself at me.

"Hi, Lizzie. Are you looking forward to the funfair?"

"Yeah. I'm going to have candy floss."

"Toffee apples are better." Mikey arrived, hot on the heels of his sister.

"I'm sure they'll have both." Kathy caught up with the kids.

"Which do you like best, Auntie Jill?" Mikey asked.

"I like them both." I was no fool. I wasn't going to pick a side, and risk upsetting one of them.

"I wasn't sure you'd show," Kathy said as we walked towards Washbridge Green.

"I said I would, didn't I?"

"Yes, but I half expected you to call and cancel because of some last-minute, urgent business."

"O ye of little faith."

"Do you blame me? It wouldn't be the first time you'd done it."

"Just don't expect me to go on any of the rides."

"Of course not. I know you're allergic to having fun."

"There's nothing fun about those rides. They're downright dangerous."

"Can I go on the waltzer, Mummy?" Lizzie yelled.

"Me too!" Mikey shouted.

"Okay, kids," Kathy said. "I'll come on with you."

"Are you coming too, Auntie Jill?" Lizzie grabbed my hand.

"Auntie Jill is too scared," Kathy said.

"You're not scared, are you, Auntie Jill?" Lizzie tugged at my hand.

"Of course not. There's nothing to be scared of."

"Come and join us, then." Kathy beckoned to me.

"Yeah!" Lizzie yelled. "Please."

"Come on, Auntie Jill!" Mikey grabbed my other hand.

Oh bum!

***

"Why are you walking funny, Auntie Jill?" Lizzie

looked concerned.

"I'm not." Why wouldn't everything stop spinning?

"You are. Isn't she, Mummy?"

"Hold on to me, Auntie Jill." Kathy took my hand. "I'll help you."

"I'm okay. I'm just a bit dizzy, that's all."

"Did you enjoy the waltzer?"

"Those stupid rides shouldn't be allowed. I feel like I've just been put through the spin cycle in my washing machine."

"You do look a little green. What you need is some candy floss."

The thought of eating candy floss, or anything else for that matter, turned my stomach.

"Would you like some, Auntie Jill?" Lizzie's mouth was already covered in the pink, gooey fluff.

"No thanks. I'm not hungry."

"Can I have a go on hook-a-duck, Mum?" Mikey said, through a mouthful of toffee apple.

"I want a go, too!" Lizzie said.

Kathy and I followed them to the hook-a-duck stall.

"Will you hold my toffee apple, Mum?" Mikey thrust the stick into Kathy's hand.

"Can you hold my candy floss, please, Auntie Jill?" Lizzie passed it to me.

Just the smell of it made my stomach churn even more. I didn't even want to look at it, so I moved my hand behind my back.

"Hey! Be careful!"

I turned around to find a bald-headed man standing behind me. His black beard was covered in pink and white candy floss.

"Sorry. I didn't see you there."

"You might have done if you'd actually looked behind you before you pushed your candy floss in my face."

He was picking the fluffy, pink and white sticky stuff out of his beard. It was going to be a long job.

I apologised again, and then shuffled over to Kathy, who was in hysterics.

"It could only happen to you, Jill."

"Isn't it time to go home, yet?"

It wasn't. I had another hour to suffer before Kathy finally called it a day.

"Okay, kids. It's time to go."

"Aww, Mummy." Lizzie pouted. "Can we stay another ten minutes?"

"I want to go on the ghost train, Mum!" Mikey tried to pull Kathy towards it.

"Okay, but after that it will be time to go home. Do you want to go on, too, Lizzie?"

"I suppose so." Lizzie didn't sound overly enthusiastic, and I wondered if that was because she was used to seeing ghosts every day.

"What about you, Jill?"

"No, thanks. I'll give this one a miss."

"Oh, yeah. I'd almost forgotten." Kathy laughed. "You're scared of ghost trains, aren't you?"

"Of course I'm not."

"You would never go on them when we were kids."

"Rubbish. There's something wrong with your memory. I just feel a little dizzy from the waltzer."

"Come on, kids. We'll leave scaredy cat, Auntie Jill, here."

She was right. I was terrified of ghost trains—I always

had been. That may sound ridiculous coming from someone who routinely spends time with 'real' ghosts, but it was true. What really got to me was the way stuff jumped out at you. My nerves couldn't stand that kind of thing.

While I was waiting for Kathy and the kids to have their final ride of the day, the bearded man walked past me, on his way to the exit. He gave me a withering look, and I could hardly blame him because he still had traces of candy floss in his beard.

"That was fantastic!" Mikey came rushing over to me. "Mum was scared, but I wasn't."

Kathy did look a little pale.

"You weren't scared, were you, Kathy?" I grinned.

"That was really horrible. Those ghosts were terrifying."

"That's because they were real ghosts, Mummy," Lizzie said, almost matter-of-factly.

Chapter 5

The next morning, over breakfast, Jack was once again engrossed in something on his phone.

"Hello? Remember me?" I waved to him across the breakfast bar.

"I've found a fancy dress shop in Washbridge. It looks like we'll get something suitable there."

"I don't need anything."

"You said you'd go to the Con."

"I didn't say I'd get dressed up in some stupid costume."

"You have to. Everyone there will be in costume. You'll stand out like a sore thumb, if you don't."

"Fine. Do they have any 'apathetic bystander' costumes?"

"I think we should go as Vamp and Champ."

"As who?"

"It's a popular TV program, apparently."

"I've never heard of it. I assume Vamp is a vampire, but what is Champ?"

"He's a vampire too. That's just his nickname. Look, this shop has vampire costumes, so we should be able to find something suitable."

"I'm not putting false fangs in my mouth."

"You have to. Vampires always have fangs."

"Since when did you become the world's leading authority on vampires?"

"It's common knowledge."

"Is it really? Did you know about the patches, too?"

"What patches?"

"Vampires use them to stave off their craving for

human blood."

"Don't be ridiculous. Where did you read that nonsense? It's a good thing one of us knows what they're talking about. If I can get away at lunch time, will you meet me at this shop?"

"Do I have a choice?"

"Not really."

"Can't I just go as a witch?"

"I've already told you that you'd make a terrible witch."

I hadn't seen Jack so excited about anything since the last time he'd bought himself a new bowling shirt. That probably didn't say much for my sex appeal.

I knew which fancy dress shop he was talking about. It was the one where Dolly's daughter, Dorothy, had worked when she first moved to Candlefield. I was fairly sure it was still managed by a wizard. I was quite looking forward to seeing his expression when Jack told him that he didn't think I'd make a very good witch.

Jack had already left for work, and I was just about to set off for the office when I heard the unmistakable sound of bagpipes. I'd grown accustomed to hearing Mr Kilbride playing from time to time, but the noise wasn't coming from his house. It appeared to be coming from somewhere up the road, and it was gradually getting louder. Then, I spotted something in the distance; it was Mr Hosey's train, Bessie. If I'd had even an ounce of sense, I would have jumped into the car, and gunned it out of there. Instead, I was transfixed by the sound of the bagpipes which was even louder now.

As Bessie came to a halt in front of our driveway, all

became clear. Seated in the second carriage was Mr Kilbride, playing the bagpipes for all he was worth. By then, the sound was deafening.

"Good morning, Jill," Mr Hosey shouted, as he climbed down from the engine.

"Morning," I shouted back.

"I'm sorry to tell you that you have missed your chance. What is it they say? You snooze, you lose."

"I don't follow."

"The advertising opportunity that you so rashly declined." He pointed to the carriages, and only then did I notice that they were carrying an advert for bagpipe lessons from Mr Kilbride. "As you can see, Mr Kilbride is making the most of his free rides on Bessie."

"Oh, well. My loss, I guess."

"Would you be interested in lessons, Jill?" Mr Kilbride put down the bagpipes.

"Thanks, but I think I'll pass. My sister might be interested though. I'll jot down her telephone number for you."

Snigger.

***

I'd just stepped into my office building when I bumped into George from I-Sweat.

"Morning, Jill. On your way to the gym?"

"Maybe later. I have a lot on today. Are you still having problems with things being moved around during the night?"

"Not for a few days, but another strange thing is happening now. Every morning when we get here, there seems to be animal hair all over the equipment."

"That is weird. What do you think it is?"

"I don't know. It's like the place has been invaded by dogs or cats during the night."

"Perhaps they're using the gym while it's closed to humans?"

He looked confused for a moment, but then smiled. "Yeah. I guess that must be it. It's a pity we can't get them to pay subscription fees."

Jules managed a 'good morning' but didn't bother to look up. She was way too engrossed in her knitting project.

As soon as I walked into my office, Winky quickly put his paws behind his back—just as he had the previous time.

"I'm not biting," I said.

"Not biting what?"

"I know you want me to ask what you have behind your back."

"There's nothing behind my back." Once again, he showed me first one empty paw and then the other. "See!"

"I believe you."

Was it possible that he really did have something of interest behind his back? No, of course he didn't. Stop it, Jill! He's just trying to make you think it's something important. Just keep ignoring him.

What? I'm allowed to talk to myself if I want to. Are you sure about that? Yes, I'm positive.

Ten minutes later, Jules came through to my office. "Jill, look, this is my competition entry."

"A tea cosy?"

"A what? No, it's a hat."

"Oh? Right. It's just that it's—err—similar to—err—"

"Has Annabel copied my hat?"

"Err—no. Not exactly."

"Are you sure? There were a couple of times that I thought I saw her looking over the top of the filing cabinet. Have you seen her competition entry?"

"Yes, she did show it to me, and it definitely isn't a hat."

"Phew! Thank goodness. So, what do you think of it?"

"It's bound to be the best hat there."

"Thanks, Jill."

Jules returned to the outer office, obviously encouraged by my endorsement.

"Why didn't you tell her?" Winky jumped onto my desk.

"Tell her what?"

"That her hat is identical to the old bag lady's tea cosy."

"They weren't that similar."

"Are you kidding? Even I could see they were the same, and I'm a cat."

Just then, my phone rang; it was a number I didn't recognise.

"Jill? It's Constance Bowler."

"Hey, Constance. Are you calling from GT?"

"Yeah. I wasn't sure if it would work or not. Mad gave me your number. I hope you don't mind."

"Not at all. What can I do for you?"

"When you were over here, we spoke about working together. Well, something has come up that I think you might be able to help us with."

"Okay. Do you want me to come over?"

"If it isn't too much trouble?"

"I've been putting in lots of practice at travelling between here and GT. It's getting easier every time. When did you want to meet?"

"I have meetings for the rest of the day. How about tomorrow morning? Say nine o' clock?"

"That works for me. Where?"

"There's a rather nice coffee shop close to the police station."

"Okay. What's it called?"

"Spooky Wooky."

I laughed. "Really?"

"Yeah. Shall I give you directions?"

"You'd better, otherwise I might never find it."

***

I'd just finished sorting my Post-It notes, by size, when Jules walked in. She was wearing her tea cosy—err—I mean, hat.

"I'm just trying it out," she said when she caught me staring at it.

"Isn't it rather hot?"

"It is a little."

"Maybe you could put a couple of holes in the sides—for ventilation?" Here's my handle; here's my spout.

"I think that would look silly."

"You could be right. Did you come in here for something?"

"Oh yeah. I almost forgot. There's a lady out there who would like to see you."

"Who is it?"

"Her name is Day. Doris, I think she said."

"Que sera sera."

"Pardon?"

"Never mind. You'd better show her in."

The woman's pale face was devoid of makeup, and she looked as though she'd been crying for hours.

"Mrs Day?"

"It's Jay, actually. Doris Jay."

"Right. Sorry. Please have a seat. Can I get you a drink?"

"No thanks. I need your help. My daughter, Kylie, has been charged with the murder of Lee Sparks."

"The DJ?"

"You've heard of him?"

"I've listened to his show a few times."

"Kylie was his girlfriend. They say she murdered him. You have to help me, Miss Gooder."

"I need you to tell me everything that has happened."

"Yesterday, at about half past seven in the evening, two police officers turned up at my door, and told me that Kylie had been charged with Lee Sparks' murder. I thought it was some kind of joke or a mistake at first, but they were deadly serious."

"And you say she was his girlfriend?"

"Supposedly, but you would never have known it from the way he carried on."

"What do you mean?"

"I know you shouldn't speak ill of the dead, but he was a horrible man. Everyone who heard him on the radio fell under his spell; I did at first. But that was just a persona. It wasn't the real man. He cheated on Kylie, and he abused her terribly."

"Physically?"

"Mental abuse, definitely, but I wouldn't be surprised if he'd hit her too. She wouldn't have told me. He could do no wrong in her eyes. She was infatuated."

"Have you been able to see your daughter since she was arrested?"

"Yes. I saw her first thing this morning for a few minutes. She was in a terrible state, as you can imagine. It broke my heart to have to leave her."

"Did she tell you anything about what happened?"

"Not much. She was too upset. Kylie said she'd gone to the radio station to see him."

"While he was on air? Was that usual?"

"She quite often sat in on his show. When she got there, she found him dead; he'd been stabbed."

"Was there anyone else in the studio?"

"I don't know. She didn't say."

"Do you know why they think your daughter did it?"

"Kylie's fingerprints were on the knife, but she's adamant that she didn't touch it."

"You said that he'd been abusive towards her. Is it possible that she just snapped, and lashed out?"

"No! Kylie wouldn't hurt a fly. And besides, she still loved him; don't ask me why."

"It's only a couple of days since the murder. It's possible the police will realise they have the wrong person."

"How? They're convinced they have their murderer. Meanwhile, Kylie is rotting in a cell. You have to help me, Miss Gooder. You have to help me to get Kylie home."

"I'll do my best. Did Kylie ever mention anyone who had reason to dislike Sparks?"

"It would be easier to list the people who liked him. He

was full of himself, and treated everyone around him like dirt. From what Kylie told me, Sparks had had run-ins with his producer and his ex-manager. But there are many others."

"Okay. The first thing I'll need to do is speak with Kylie. Do you have a lawyer?"

"Yes. My brother-in-law is a lawyer."

"Good. Ask him to make arrangements for me to see Kylie. He may need to accompany me."

"Okay. I'll do that, and then call you later."

Chapter 6

Oh bum!

I'd promised Jack that I would meet him outside the fancy dress shop at half past one, but by the time Doris Jay had left, it was already a quarter to two.

I hurried over there, and arrived just as Jack was setting off in the opposite direction.

"Jack!"

"We said one-thirty!" He tapped his watch.

"Sorry. A new client came in without an appointment."

"Fair enough. I've still got thirty minutes. That should be long enough."

The shop wasn't exactly doing a roaring trade; we were the only customers in there.

"Hi, I'm Neil. I'm the manager. Is there anything in particular you're looking for?"

"We're going to SupsCon," Jack said.

"We've had a lot of customers in this week who are going there." He turned to me and winked. "I assume you'll be wanting a witch's outfit?"

Before I could respond, Jack jumped in, "No. We decided Jill would make a terrible witch."

We decided? I must have missed the part where I had a say in it.

"I see what you mean." The manager grinned at me.

Jack continued, "We thought we'd go as Vamp and Champ."

"Vampires, eh? Good choice. Our vampire costumes and accessories are over there, just beyond the werewolf section. If you need any help, just give me a shout."

"See, I told you," Jack said, once the manager had gone

back behind the counter. "He agreed with me that you'd make a terrible witch."

"Let's just pick a costume, and get out of here. I've got a lot of work on."

"We have to look the part. You can't rush these things."

He wasn't kidding. He tried on practically every so-called vampire costume in the shop. They were, of course, all totally ridiculous. I'd seen any number of vampires, and not one of them had been wearing a long, black cape.

"I think this is the one." Jack was admiring himself in the full-length mirror. "And what about these?" He turned around and flashed his 'fangs'.

"Plastic teeth? Very realistic."

"Of course they're not realistic. Vampires aren't real."

"Sorry. I forgot. Now, can we go?"

"What about *your* costume?"

"This one will do."

"But that's the only one you've tried on."

"This one is fine. Let's pay for them and get out of here. I'm starving."

"Hold on. You need some fangs."

"I'm not putting those things in my mouth."

"You have to. How can you be a vampire without fangs?"

"Okay, okay." I picked up a set of the plastic fangs. "Happy now?"

"We need some blood."

"What?"

"Look. They have pouches of fake blood. We can put some on our chins. It will make it look like we've just been sucking blood."

When Jack did something, he didn't do it by halves.

When we came to pay, the manager gave me another sly wink. "You'll make a great vampire. You're a natural."

He was enjoying this way too much.

As soon as we got out of the shop, Jack had to rush off. I grabbed a sandwich, and walked over to Ever where Kathy and Chloe were both running around like headless chickens.

"Hi!" I called to Kathy.

"Hey, Jill. I didn't see you there."

"You look busy."

"It's getting ridiculous. We're somehow meant to run the shop, the tea room and the roof terrace. And on top of that, we have all the general duties—like checking orders sent via the website."

"What about Grandma? What does she do all day?"

"That's a very good question. You should ask her."

"No thanks. She's already on my case about the tax."

"What is this tax she keeps going on about?"

Oh bum! I really should engage my brain before speaking. I could hardly tell Kathy about the new tax being proposed in the supernatural world, could I?

"Tax? Oh, wait. Did you think she meant *tax* as in what we have to pay to the government?"

"What else?"

"She was talking about *tacks*—the sharp, pointy things. I was putting up a picture, and I dropped one. Grandma trod on it, and she was hopping mad."

"Right?" Kathy gave me her '*at least we aren't related by blood*' look. "By the way, I'm not the only one who's fed up with all the work we have to do. Chloe is cheesed off as well, and she's only been here for five minutes."

"You know what you should both do, don't you?"

"What?"

"Go on strike for more money."

"You know what, Jill? That's actually not a bad idea. In fact, it's a great idea."

"It was only a joke. I wasn't seriously suggesting—"

But Kathy had already walked away; she was headed towards Chloe.

While I was on the high street, I called in at WashBets. It was the same woman behind the counter as on my previous visit—she still looked dead inside.

"I'd like to speak to Ryan, please."

"If it's a complaint, you need to speak to his assistant, Bryan."

"So you mentioned the last time I was in here. This is a personal matter."

"Are you his girlfriend?"

The woman obviously had the memory of an elephant—a dead one.

"No, I'm not his girlfriend, but if you could just tell him I need to talk to him about Megan."

"Megan? Is that you?"

"No. That's his girlfriend."

"I thought you said you weren't his girlfriend?"

Oh boy! This woman really should get together with Norman.

Eventually, I got to speak to Ryan.

"Has your assistant been working here long?"

"Tonya? Yeah, she's an absolute genius."

"I can tell." I laughed. "A real mastermind."

"I'm being serious. She's a mathematical whizz. She can work out odds and payments in her head faster than any computer. I don't know how I'd cope without her. Anyway, why are you here? I've been wearing the patches, and there's been no—err—you know—funny business."

"I know. Megan seems a lot happier."

"So why are you here?"

"Megan had a word with me. She asked if I knew anything about teeth."

"I don't understand."

"It seems that your fangs are freaking her out a little."

"Oh no. It's not deliberate, I promise. It's more of a reflex. I'm not even aware it's happening. What did she say?"

"She thinks you have some weird wisdom teeth thing going on."

"I don't want to lose her, but I don't know what I can do about the fangs."

"I may be able to help there." I took out the note that Alan had given to me, and handed it to Ryan.

"StopFangs? What's this?"

"I'm surprised you haven't heard of it. Apparently, it's used by a lot of vampires who live in the human world. I don't know exactly how it works, but it's specifically designed to stop your fangs from making an appearance."

"That's great, thanks. Do you know where I can find it?"

"According to my contact, you can get it in any pharmacy in Candlefield."

"Thanks, Jill. You're a life-saver."

"Before you start to use it, you'd better tell Megan you have to pay a visit to the dentist to sort out your 'wisdom teeth'. If you don't, she's going to wonder what's happened to them."

"Good idea. Thanks."

As I made my way back up the high street, I noticed that Top Of The World was doing a roaring trade. Norman was standing outside, enjoying a sausage roll.

"Tea break, Norman?"

As usual, it took a couple of minutes for the cogs to click into place.

"I don't like tea."

"Right, but you're on a break?"

"Yeah. I'm eating a sausage roll."

"So I see. Tell me, Norman, do you ever place a bet?"

"What on?"

"Anything. Horses, greyhounds, football?"

"I once placed a bet on the Eurovision Song Contest."

"Did you win?"

"No. They came last."

"Nul point, eh?"

"No, they didn't get any points."

"Right. You should drop into WashBets when you're next passing. The woman who works there, Tonya, is really — err — nice."

"Does she like bottle tops?"

"That subject hasn't come up in our conversations so far, but I'd say she definitely has the potential to."

"Okay. I might do that."

What? There's nothing wrong with giving love a little nudge. And anyway, you should know by now that I'm just an old romantic at heart.

***

I was still hungry, so I decided to magic myself over to Candlefield. I fancied a muffin, but for once, I wouldn't be purchasing it from Cuppy C.

"A caramel latte and a blueberry muffin, please."

"What are you doing in here?" Flora looked at me as though I was something smelly that she'd just trodden in.

"Last time I checked, this was a tea room, and I believe Miles told you that I'd be coming in."

"Look what the cat dragged in," Flora called to Laura.

"Lost your way?" Laura joined her fellow ice maiden behind the counter.

"Are you going to serve me or not?"

"I suppose you want a giant muffin?"

"Is there any other size?"

Flora took one out of the display cabinet, and dropped it onto the plate.

Moments later, Laura thumped the cup down on the counter, causing the coffee to slop over the top.

"That will be eight pounds sixty-three."

"That's outrageous."

"Take it or leave it."

I took it, and found a seat at a table where I could keep a close watch on proceedings. The coffee was just about okay, but the muffin wasn't a patch on the ones from Cuppy C. Still, I somehow managed to force it down.

After about fifteen minutes, Flora disappeared into the back, and then reappeared a few minutes later. She was carrying a tray full of cakes, which she placed in the display cabinet.

That was what I'd been waiting to see.

"Going so soon?" Laura called after me as I made my way to the door.

"Lovely to see you, Jill." Flora cackled.

Part of me hoped that Mindy was right, and that the ice maidens were behind the sabotage. Nothing would have given me greater pleasure than to bust their sorry backsides.

"Traitor!" Pearl yelled at me as soon as I walked through the door of Cuppy C.

"We saw you!" Amber shot me a frosty look. "Aren't our muffins good enough for you now?"

"It's not what it looks like."

"It looks like you've just had coffee and a muffin with the enemy, and now you've come for another helping."

"I'm disappointed in you both. You should know I would never desert Cuppy C for Best Cakes. I'm working on a case. The only reason I was in there was to carry out surveillance."

"Is it something involving Miles Best?" Amber said. "Are you going to bust him?"

"I can't discuss the case; you know that."

I didn't dare tell them that Miles Best was my client. They would have banned me from Cuppy C for life if they'd known that I was working for their sworn enemy.

"What are their muffins like?" Pearl asked.

"Not great. Yours are much better. So is your coffee."

That brought a smile back to their faces.

Cuppy C was busy, but nowhere near as busy as the day before.

"How come you two are working in here today, anyway?"

"Why wouldn't we be?" Pearl shrugged.

"I thought Alan and William were supposed to be in here for three days?"

"We had to step in," Amber said. "The guys simply couldn't cope."

Huh?

"I've been in here the last two days, and both times they seemed to be doing just fine. They're both whizzes on the coffee machine."

"Appearances can be deceptive," Pearl said. "And, let's be honest, Jill. You're hardly qualified to judge."

"And besides," Amber chipped in. "Takings were way down."

That couldn't possibly be true. The shop had been buzzing on both days. I was beginning to smell a rat.

"It couldn't have anything to do with how much female attention the guys were getting, could it? Did the green-eyed monster come knocking?"

"Don't be ridiculous!" Pearl scoffed. "Why would we be jealous?"

"Of course not," Amber said. "We just did what was best for the shop."

"Excuse me?" A young woman interrupted. She was with three other women of a similar age.

"What can I get you?" Amber put on her 'customer-facing' smile.

"We don't want to order anything. We were just wondering when the two guys, who were working in here yesterday, would be in again?"

The look on the twins' faces was priceless.

Chapter 7

"Do you have to do that while I'm eating my breakfast?" I said.

Jack was sitting at the breakfast bar, trying out his plastic fangs.

"I want to make sure they're comfortable for the big day."

Big day? "It's putting me off my cornflakes."

Before he could respond, his phone rang. What ensued was pretty hilarious because the fangs had obviously become wedged in his mouth, so he was forced to speak with them still in place.

"Hleloo." He slobbered into the phone. "Yles. It's Mle Mlum. Yles, I'm oklay. Jlust a mlinute."

By now, I was helpless with laughter.

Jack put the phone down while he wrestled with the fangs. After a couple of minutes, he finally managed to get them out.

"It isn't funny, Jill."

I still couldn't speak for laughing.

"Hello, Mum. Sorry about that. I was choking on my muesli. Yes, I'm okay now. The laughter? That was Jill. No, she wasn't laughing at me choking. She's watching something on YouTube."

I somehow managed to pull myself together while Jack continued with the call.

"Yes, Mum, I'm sure. We'd love to have you. Okay, see you then. Love you, bye." He finished the call, and then turned to me. "Have you done with the hilarity?"

I most definitely had. Just as soon as I'd heard the words: *We'd love to have you.*

"What did she want?"

"She's going to come and stay with us for a couple of days."

"Why?"

"What do you mean, '*why*'? Does she need a reason?"

"I knew it. I told you, didn't I?"

"Told me what?"

"Your mother hates me. She's coming down here to try to break us up."

"Why would she want to do that? You're being crazy. She probably just wants to see the house."

"Didn't you see the way she avoided me at the anniversary party?"

"No, I didn't, and I'm absolutely sure that was just a figment of your imagination."

"When is she coming?"

"On Monday."

"Which Monday?"

"Next Monday."

"How long for?"

"Just a couple of days."

"Maybe I should go and stay with Kathy while she's here?"

"You're being ridiculous. It will be fine. Mum will love you when she gets to know you." He pulled me into his arms, and gave me a kiss. "Just like I do."

As soon as Jack had left for work, I called Kathy.

"She's coming here!"

"Slow down, Jill. Who's coming?"

"Jack's mother. She's coming to stay on Monday."

"That will be nice for you both. Is his dad coming too?

We could all have lunch together."

"Never mind lunch. Didn't you hear what I said? She's obviously coming down here to split us up."

"Now you're being stupid. I hope you haven't said any of this to Jack."

"Of course I have."

"Oh boy. It's a good thing he's crazy about you, or he'd run a mile."

"Maybe you're right. I'm probably worrying about nothing."

"You think?"

"I'd better let you get ready for work."

"There's no hurry; I'm not going in. We took your advice."

"What advice?"

"To go on strike. Chloe and I walked out yesterday afternoon. We're going to stay out until your grandmother gives us a pay rise."

"I was only joking about going on strike."

"You were right. We've let your grandmother push us around for far too long."

"Fair enough, but—err—you didn't happen to mention to Grandma that I was the one who had suggested it, did you?"

"Of course I did. I told her that you thought we were being exploited, and should withdraw our labour."

Oh bum!

***

The receptionist-count that morning was two. As soon as I walked through the door, Mrs V held up her tea cosy.

"It's finished."

"Very nice."

"Mine is finished too." Jules held up her hat.

Neither of them could see the other one's masterpiece because of the filing cabinet which was in between their desks. Little did they realise that they'd used almost identical patterns. At first glance, they both looked like hats. Or was it tea cosies? I had a horrible feeling that this wasn't going to end well.

"They're both equally terrific," I said. "Good luck to both of you."

Winky was once again talking to Bob the spider. They were both seated on the sofa.

"How's Bob this morning?" I felt like I should ask.

"His arthritis is giving him gyp."

"Spiders don't get arthritis."

"Are you suggesting Bob would lie about something like that?"

"No — err — of course not."

"We were discussing music."

"Is he a fan of Ziggy Stardust?"

"Who?"

"Never mind. Before your time."

"He's into grunge."

"Nice."

Half way through the morning, Mrs V came through to my office.

"There's a gentleman out there who is asking if you could spare him a few minutes."

"What's his name?"

"I'm not sure because he mumbles. Mr Dings, I think. Ed Dings."

"Okay, send him in."

There was something rather strange about Mr Dings, and I knew exactly what it was: the false beard and moustache.

"Mr Dings?"

"Actually, my name is Heddings."

"Oh? Sorry. Do have a seat, Mr Heddings. How can I help?"

As he sat down, the moustache became dislodged and fell into his lap. He quickly snatched it up, and stuck it back onto his top lip, while pretending to sneeze. Wow! This guy was a real pro.

"I need something investigating." His gaze drifted all around the room — everywhere but at me.

"You're going to have to be a little more specific."

"Something has happened, and I need you to investigate it."

Just then, Winky, who had been asleep, emerged from under the sofa.

Heddings' gaze immediately locked onto the cat, and suddenly everything made sense.

"I think I must have dropped my wallet." Heddings patted his coat pocket. What a thesp this guy was.

"Oh dear." I played along.

"Maybe I dropped it in your reception area? Would you check for me?"

"Certainly, Mr Heddings. You stay there."

I walked over to the door, and opened and closed it without actually stepping out of the office. Because Heddings was as dumb as a stick of rhubarb, he didn't think to look over his shoulder, to check I'd actually left the room. Instead, he took out his phone, and snapped a picture of Winky.

I opened and closed the door again.

"There's no sign of your wallet out there, Mr Heddings."

"Never mind." He shoved the phone back into his pocket, and stood up. "I have to get going."

"What about the thing that you wanted investigating?"

"Huh? Oh, that? It's okay now."

I'd had enough of this imbecile, so I cast the 'freeze' spell. While he was immobilised, I took out his phone, and deleted the most recent photograph. I then stuck out my tongue, and took a selfie on his phone. After replacing the phone, I reversed the 'freeze' spell.

"Bye then, Mr Heddings."

"Bye," he said while holding his moustache in place.

What a cheapskate Gordon Armitage was. Where had he found that pathetic excuse for a P.I?

***

It was time for my meeting with Constance Bowler. I was getting much better at transporting myself to Ghost Town, but it still took a little more concentration than when magicking myself to Candlefield.

She'd given me directions to her favourite coffee shop, Spooky Wooky.

Best. Name. Ever.

I'd half-expected it to be ghost-themed, but in fact it was like an overdose of floral. The wallpaper had a floral pattern, the tablecloths too, and the middle-aged man behind the counter wore a floral-patterned apron.

"Jill!" Constance, who had been seated at a table close to the counter, came over to greet me. "Did you get over here okay?"

"Yeah. I think I've mastered it now. I just need to learn to find my way around GT. It's much bigger than I expected."

"What do you think of this place?"

"It's nice. Very — err — floral."

"Hi." The man behind the counter had an impressive moustache — this one wasn't false. "You must be Jill. We've heard a lot about you."

"And your love of blueberry muffins." A second man appeared behind the counter. He was completely bald; his head had been polished to an impressive shine.

"Who told you?"

"Mad is a regular in here," the bald man said. "She told us we'd need to stock up on blueberry muffins, and that we'd better make sure they were big ones."

"In that case, it would be rude not to try one. By the way, I love the name of this place. It's very ghostly."

"Sorry?"

They both looked puzzled.

"Spooky Wooky — it's very ghostly."

"Oh?" the bald man said. "Now you come to mention it, I suppose it is."

Huh? Colour me confused.

"The shop's name actually comes from their names," Constance said.

"I'm Harry Wook." The bald man offered his hand.

"And I'm Larry Spooks." The moustached man did likewise.

"I see. What do I call you both? Spooky and Wooky?"

"Harry and Larry will be fine." Larry passed me a plate. "There you go. GT's finest blueberry muffin. You must let us know what you think of it."

"Thanks. It looks delicious."

And it was. Maybe not quite as good as those in Cuppy C, but it was a close-run thing.

"The guys seem nice," I said, once Constance and I were seated at the table.

"They're lovely. They bake all their own cakes."

"Really? That is impressive. I assumed they bought them in."

"They ran a small bakery together in the human world until they both died in a fire. From what I hear, arson was suspected."

"That's terrible."

"Still, the human world's loss is GT's gain."

"You said there was something I could help you with?"

"I hope so. It's a particularly nasty business. I assume you're familiar with human trafficking?"

"Of course. It's a terrible trade in human misery."

"Unfortunately, trafficking isn't restricted to only the human world. Ghosts are being trafficked from here to Washbridge and beyond."

"I'm sorry. I don't really understand."

"The majority of ghosts are quite content to live here in GT. Others prefer to spend some of their time in the human world—usually with relatives or friends. Humans would normally refer to this as a haunting."

"You mean like when my mother attaches herself to me?"

"Precisely. Problems arise when a ghost wants to visit

the human world but doesn't have anyone to whom they can attach themselves. Those are the ghosts that the traffickers prey upon. They promise to provide them with a human host."

"In return for a fee, I assume?"

"An exorbitant fee. That's despicable enough, but it doesn't end there. Many ghosts who have paid for this 'service' have simply disappeared. They've never been seen again."

"That's terrible."

"Which is where you come in. Until now, we've had no way of tracing what was happening to the ghosts who paid to use the service. I'm hoping you might be able to find out what's happening to them in the human world."

"I'll certainly give it a go. I hate to think of anyone, human or ghost, being treated like that. I'm going to need a lot more information than you've given me so far, though."

"Of course. I'd like you to meet Bertie Myflowers. He paid to use the service, but then got cold feet at the last minute."

"It sounds as though he was lucky."

"Definitely. He should be a good starting point for your investigation."

"When can I meet with him?"

"I need to talk to him first, to set it up. I'll give you a call."

"Great."

Chapter 8

After I'd finished my meeting with Constance, I decided to take a short walk around Ghost Town. Ten minutes from the coffee shop, I came across the market place, which was even bigger than the one in Washbridge, and just as busy.

"Jill!" It was my father; he was with Blodwyn. "Your mother told me that you'd found a way to transport yourself here, but I didn't believe her because she likes to wind me up. How did you manage it?"

"A lot of painful trial and error." I glanced at the bags they were carrying. "Looks like you've been busy."

"It's our weekly shop." Blodwyn's accent was as delightful as ever. "What do you make of the market, Jill?"

"I've only just got here, but it seems mighty impressive."

"It is. You should take a good look around. We can't hang around, unfortunately." My father held up one of the bags. "Some of this stuff needs to go into the freezer. But now you're able to come to GT, why don't you join us for Sunday lunch, this weekend?"

"That would be nice, thanks. I already know where to find you. Yours is the house that is painted red, right?"

"I take it that your mother has been complaining about the colour?"

"She's not impressed."

"We only did it to wind her up."

"Less of the 'we'." Blodwyn play-thumped his arm. "I had nothing to do with it, Jill. Those two are as bad as one another."

"I'd better let you get your frozen stuff home. I'll see you both on Sunday."

When Mad had first floated the idea of my magicking myself to GT, it had seemed rather far-fetched. Even after I'd managed to do it, I'd only really considered how it might help with inter-world crime fighting. I was just beginning to realise that it would also enable me to reconnect with my birth parents and their families. It was such a shame that I couldn't share any of this with Jack.

***

Doris Jay had contacted me to confirm that her brother-in-law, Charles Parsons, the solicitor, had arranged for me to talk to Kylie. I'd expected another run-in with Leo Riley, but when I met Parsons at Washbridge police station, we were shown straight to an interview room by the duty sergeant—there was no sign of Riley.

Doris had told me that her daughter was twenty-three years old, but she looked older—the events of the last few days had obviously taken their toll. Her lank, mousy hair fell over her face, obscuring her eyes.

"Kylie, this is Jill Gooder." Parsons introduced me. "Your mum has hired her to help with your case."

"Hi, Kylie," I said. "Are you okay to answer my questions?"

"I guess." She shrugged.

"How are you feeling?"

"How do you think?" She suddenly became animated. "It's horrible in here. Can you get me out?"

"Only the courts can decide that," Parsons interjected.

"There's a good chance you will get bail."

"I can't stay here for another night. I'll go crazy."

"Kylie!" I raised my voice to get her attention. "I know this is a nightmare for you, but we only have a limited amount of time. If I'm going to help you, I really do need you to answer my questions."

"Okay."

"Can you start by telling me exactly what happened when you walked into the studio?"

"Lee was just sitting there—staring at me. I didn't realise anything was wrong at first—not until I saw—" She paused for a moment to compose herself. "The blood. And the knife."

"Was there anyone else in the studio?"

She shook her head.

"What about on your way in? Did you pass anyone?"

"No."

"Did you touch the knife?"

"No!" She shouted. "Why does everyone keep asking me that?"

"You were in shock. Is it possible that your hand went to the knife, instinctively?"

"No. As soon as I saw the blood and the knife, I just screamed and backed away."

"Okay. Can we talk about your relationship with Lee Sparks?"

"I loved him. I used to call him Sparky, and he called me Little Jay."

"Did he love you?"

"Yes." She looked down at the table. "At first."

"But that changed?"

"He still insisted he loved me—"

"But?"

"He was seeing other girls." She looked up again. "He denied it, but I knew he was."

"Your mother said he treated you badly. Was he ever violent towards you?"

"No." She hesitated. "Not really. He just had a short fuse."

"But you still loved him?"

"I know you think I'm stupid."

"I'm not here to pass judgement on you. I'm here to try to help. Why did you visit the studio that day?"

"We'd had a fight the night before. I'd walked out on him."

"Were you there to try to make up?"

"No. I'd gone there to finish with him, once and for all. Even though I still loved him, I'd realised that he was never going to change."

"How did he react?"

"He didn't!" She glared at me. "I've already told you. Lee was dead when I got there."

"Were you expecting him to take it badly? Is that why you took the knife with you?"

She pushed the chair back, and stood up. "I thought you were here to help me? I didn't take the knife, and I didn't kill Lee."

"I believe you, but I had to be sure. Sit down again, please."

She took a deep breath to compose herself before returning to her seat.

"What I need you to do now, Kylie, is to give me the names of everyone who had a grudge against Lee. Anyone you can think of."

"A lot of people didn't like Lee. He was arrogant, and didn't care about anyone except himself." She caught my look. "I know what you're thinking. Why would I want to be with someone like that?"

"That doesn't matter."

"I'll tell you why. When we first met, he treated me like a princess. He made me feel like I was the only person in the world who mattered to him."

"You said there were a lot of people who didn't like Lee. Who in particular?"

"He'd recently sacked his manager, Raymond Conway. Lee said he was useless. Ray threatened Lee with all kinds of stuff."

"Did Lee seem worried?"

"No. He just brushed it off. Then there's Mike Spins."

"Who's he?"

"Another DJ at the radio station. He used to have the drive-time spot before they brought Lee in. Mike is like a thousand years old — a has-been, according to Lee."

"Anyone else?"

"Dale Royal?"

"Who's that?"

"The producer. Lee didn't rate him, and was going to bring in his own man."

"What would that have meant for Royal?"

"I'm not sure. He'd probably have been out of a job."

"Anyone else?"

"No, I don't think so." She hesitated. "There was the stalker, of course."

"What stalker?"

"She called herself a super-fan, and used to hang around the radio station all the time. She was convinced that Lee was in love with her. At first, Lee thought it was funny, but after a while he got fed up with it. He ended up taking out a restraining order against her."

"Do you know her name?"

"Hills. Short for Hilary, I think. I don't know her last name."

"No problem. I'll find her."

"Can you help to clear my name? I don't want to go to prison for something I didn't do."

"Don't worry. I'll find out who murdered Lee."

***

I wasn't looking forward to this. It was the meeting of the Combined Sup Council, and I was under pressure to try to stop them passing the new tax on sups living in the human world.

I was just about to go into the town hall when my phone rang. It was Grandma—just what I needed.

"I can't talk now, Grandma. I'm just about to go into the meeting."

"What meeting?"

"What do you mean: *what meeting*? The one you've been on my case about for the last week. The vote on the new tax proposal."

"Oh, yes. I'd forgotten that was today. Just make sure the vote goes the right way."

"I'll try. I have to get inside now."

"Hold your horses, young lady. I have a bone to pick with you."

"This is hardly the time, Grandma. I'm going to be late."

"How dare you incite my staff to strike?"

"I don't know what you mean."

"Don't play the innocent with me. I know it was you who gave them the idea. Your sister and Chloe are standing outside my shop, brandishing placards. I'm all by myself in here. How am I supposed to cope?"

"You'll just have to negotiate with them."

"Do what? Do you think I'm going to be bullied by those two?"

"They're not bullying you, Grandma. They simply want a fair wage for a fair day's work."

"We'll see how they feel when I bring in new staff. They'll be laughing on the other side of their faces then."

"Can't you just be reasonable?"

"Reasonable?" She cackled. "What a ridiculous idea. Now get in there and get that tax proposal thrown out."

Oh dear. I'd really done it this time. When I'd suggested the strike to Kathy, I hadn't thought she'd actually go through with it. If she and Chloe lost their jobs, I'd be in big trouble.

***

I hated the meetings of the Combined Sup Council. Most of the time was spent discussing trivial matters, which were of little or no importance to anyone outside those four walls. The majority of members on the council were so full of their own self-importance that it was actually painful.

I sat through the first nine items on the agenda, without saying a word. It took me all my time not to doze off.

"And now we come to the final item on today's agenda," the chairman said. "The proposal to introduce a tax on sups living in the human world. I'm sure everyone around this table will agree this is long overdue, so unless there are any objections, I suggest we go straight to a vote."

"Wait!" I stood up.

All eyes were on me.

"Miss Gooder?" The chairman smiled that charming but false smile of his. "Was there something you wanted to say?"

"Yes, actually. I wanted to congratulate all the members around this table for their selflessness today. All too often, politicians avoid passing any regulation that will adversely affect the constituents whose votes they rely on. I am impressed by your conviction to do what is right, regardless of the impact that may have on your chances of being re-elected. I'm sure you will all be aware that there are a large number of sups who live and work in the human world. Each of those sups is of course entitled to vote in the elections. It's true that normally very few bother to do so because they are not affected by the council's policies as much as those who live in Candlefield. The proposed tax is different because it will affect every one of them. Come the next election, we'd be naive to believe that they won't want to express their anger by voting against those council members who helped to introduce the new tax. Still, as I've already said, I can't help but admire your integrity for pushing this through. So, let's take a vote. I vote for the new tax." I raised my hand.

The chairman, along with everyone else around the table, looked stunned. "Err—thank you, Miss Gooder. All those in favour of the new tax, please raise your hand."

Mine was the only hand raised.

Chapter 9

When we came out of the town hall, I was giddy with delight. Me, the politician? Who would have thought it? As soon as I was out of earshot of the other council members, I made a call to Grandma. She would be thrilled with the news.

"Grandma, it's me."

"Of course it's you. Who else would it be on your phone?"

"I have good news."

"I could do with some."

"The new tax proposal was defeated. I managed to talk them around."

"Good, now how about talking your sister around. She's still on strike."

"Is that all the thanks I get?"

"I'm sorry, Jill. That was very thoughtless of me. Maybe you'd like me to bake you a cake? Would you like a chocolate one? Or maybe, a nice strawberry one? How about some champagne too?"

"A 'thank you' would be nice. It wouldn't kill you to show a little gratitude."

"Hold on a second, Jill. I think I just heard something. Oh, it's okay. It was just the sound of a tiny violin. Can you hear it?"

"Goodbye!" I ended the call.

That woman was the most selfish, despicable person I'd ever known. Just wait until she wanted another favour from me. I'd tell her to go whistle.

What do you mean 'talk is cheap'? You just see if I don't.

"Whatever is wrong, Jill?" Aunt Lucy was in her kitchen.

"It's Grandma."

"I might have known. What has she done this time?"

"She's been banging on at me for ages to get the new tax proposal thrown out at the Combined Sup Council meeting. Somehow, against all the odds, I managed to do it, and what thanks do I get?"

"None, I'm guessing?"

"Not even so much as a 'thank you'. To hear her talk, you'd have thought *she* was doing *me* a favour."

"I don't really understand why you're surprised. Surely, you know her well enough by now."

"You're right, but every now and then, I delude myself into believing that maybe, somewhere deep inside, she has a heart."

"How about a nice cup of tea and some custard creams? That'll cheer you up."

"Thanks. The thing I don't understand is, with Grandma for a mother, how did you and Mum turn out so nice?"

"Maybe we'll turn bitter and twisted when we get older, too."

"I doubt that."

By the time I'd eaten my fourth custard cream, I was beginning to calm down.

What do you mean, greedy? There were extenuating circumstances.

"I was going to ask you a favour, Jill, but I'm not sure I

should after your run in with Grandma."

"Don't be silly. You can ask me anything. I owe you so much."

"I could do with some help to pick out a dress for the grim reaper dinner and dance."

"Wouldn't you be better asking the twins?"

"No. They'd try to persuade me to buy something that *they* like, but that doesn't suit me at all. The difficulty is knowing what would be appropriate for a grim reaper bash. Does everyone dress like they would for any other dinner and dance, or do you think people stick with drab colours?"

"I hadn't considered that."

"Will you help me to choose something?"

"Sure."

"Thanks, Jill. And don't mention it to the twins, please."

"My lips are sealed. Talking of 'sealed', do you know what happened to Magna's room at the museum?"

"I heard that they'd resealed it. They didn't want visitors to the museum going down there. Why do you ask?"

"Do you remember I told you about Imelda Barrowtop's journal?"

"Yes. I didn't think you had it, though?"

"I do now, thanks to the starlight fairy wings which you found for me."

"Is there anything in there of interest?"

"Nothing much." I lied because I didn't want to freak Aunt Lucy out by telling her about the red haired, red bearded man, or about the pendant. "But there is mention that Magna left some kind of message inside the sealed room."

"What kind of message?"

"I've no idea. I'd like to take a look inside to see if I can find it."

"I know I said the room had been resealed, but I'm sure they wouldn't object to you going back inside."

"I'll go over there when I get the chance. It's probably nothing, but it can't do any harm to take a look around."

"Did you go and see Miles Best?" Aunt Lucy took a new packet of custard creams out of the cupboard, to replenish the Tupperware box.

"Yes. In fact, I wanted to talk to you about that. I wondered how you'd feel about helping me with that particular case?"

"Me? Help you with a case?" Her face lit up. "How exciting! What would you need me to do?"

I spent the next twenty minutes running through my plan with her.

"What do you think? Are you up for it?"

"Count me in, Jill. When do we do it?"

***

Mrs V didn't look happy; neither did Jules.

"Have you two fallen out again?"

"Not with each other."

They were both glaring at me.

"Hang on. Are you both mad at me? What did I do?"

"Why didn't you tell us, Jill?" Jules demanded.

"Why didn't I tell you what?"

"That we were both making the same thing?" Mrs V said.

"Hold on! You both made it quite clear that I wasn't to

tell the other what you were making. And besides, they're not the same. Yours is a tea cosy, and Jules' is a hat."

"They're the same design—using the same pattern. They're almost identical."

Mrs V stood up and held her tea cosy aloft. Jules followed suit, and held up her hat. There was very little difference between them.

"Couldn't one of you knit something else for the competition?"

"There isn't time." Mrs V's frustration was showing. "The entries have to be submitted by this evening."

"Right, sorry. I don't really know what to say, then."

That was me off their Christmas card list.

I'd just set foot in my office when Winky screamed at me, "Get back!"

"What?" I stepped back.

He reached down and scooped something off the floor. "You've killed him!"

"Killed who?"

"Bob! You just stood on him. Murderer!" Winky scurried away, and hid under the sofa.

"Winky! I'm sorry. I didn't see him there."

"He was my only friend." He was fighting back the tears. "Bob's gone. Who will I talk to now?"

"I'm really sorry. It was an accident. Please, come out from under there."

"I'm never coming out again. There's nothing left for me now."

"Don't say that. I'm sure there are other spiders in here."

"Do you think Bob can be replaced just like that? Do

you think he's interchangeable?"

"No, of course not. That's not what I meant." I felt dreadful. "Look, why don't you have some salmon? That might make you feel a little better."

"I'm really upset. It will take a lot of salmon to ease the pain."

"Of course. How does a double-helping sound?"

"It's a start, I guess. Anything to take my mind off the pain of losing Bob."

Once I'd put the salmon into his bowl, he came out from under the sofa, but deliberately didn't make eye contact with me. Hopefully, time and plenty of salmon would get him through this difficult period.

***

After work, as I was walking back to the car, my phone rang. It was Constance Bowler.

"Jill, I've been in touch with Bertie Myflowers. He was a bit freaked out when I told him that he'd be talking to a sup, but he's happy to see you. Is there any chance you could meet with him tomorrow?"

"Sure."

She gave me his address, and I promised to go and see him the next day.

"Hi, Jill!"

It was Luther. Maria was on his arm, and they both looked very happy.

"Hey, you two. I guess I don't need to ask if things are going well."

"We're very grateful to you, Jill," Luther said. "Aren't

we, Maria?"

"Very." Maria patted her upper arm surreptitiously, and I realised that was where she'd attached the synthetic blood patch.

"The four of us should have dinner again some time." Luther suggested.

"That would be nice. I'll talk to Jack."

"And don't forget that it's the end of the tax year soon." He was back in accountant mode.

"Goody, goody. My favourite time of the year."

***

When I arrived home, Megan came over to see me.

"Great news, Jill. Ryan is going to get those weird teeth of his sorted out at the dentist."

"Did you have a word with him about them?"

"No, of course not. I didn't want to embarrass him. It's weird—it's like we're telepathic—like he knew what I was thinking. I guess that's a good thing in a relationship, isn't it? Does Jack often know what you're thinking?"

"I can't say he does." Thank goodness. "It's great news about Ryan's fangs."

She looked aghast.

"Sorry. Did I just say fangs? I meant teeth. I'm glad he's getting them seen to."

Jack was already home. I could tell he was bursting to tell me something as soon as I walked through the door.

"I have good news!" he announced. "Times two."

"Has your mother decided not to come over?"

"No. How would that be good news? I've got tickets for

the Combined Forces Dinner and Dance."

"For the *what*?"

"Washbridge and West Chipping hold a combined dinner and dance every year."

Whoop-de-doo!

He continued, "When I joined West Chipping, the tickets had all been sold, so I didn't mention it to you because I knew you'd be disappointed."

Devastated. "What's changed?"

"Someone had to drop out at the last minute, so they offered the tickets to me. Great, eh?"

"Great. When you say, 'last minute', exactly how last minute is it?"

"The dance is next Wednesday, so we still have a little time to practise."

"Practise what?"

"Our dancing, of course."

"It's not a competition, is it?"

"No, but I have my reputation to think of."

"*Reputation*?" I tried, but failed to stifle a laugh. "Sorry."

"People know I've won competitions. They'll expect high standards. It's okay, though, we can put in some practice every evening between now and then."

Oh goody. "You said 'times two'. Is your second piece of good news as exciting as the first?"

"Even more so. Come and look at this." He led the way into the lounge where he had his laptop open on the coffee table. "Look! I've found a ticket for the 'We' concert. You'll be able to come with us."

If this was more good news, I didn't want to be around when Jack had bad news.

"Hmm? I'd love to go, obviously, but it wouldn't be the

same if I can't sit with the three of you."

"That's not a problem."

"It isn't?"

"Didn't you know? The three tickets we already have are for the standing area. We couldn't get any seats. This ticket is in 'standing' too, so we'll all be together."

"Standing?"

"Great, isn't it?"

"For an hour and a half?"

"Three hours if you include the support acts."

"Fantastic!"

"I do have some slightly bad news though," he said.

I wasn't sure I could handle any more. "What's that?"

"The cleaner called by just before you got home."

"Mrs Crustie? Has she quit?"

"No. She said she has to increase her rates."

"I hope you told her to get stuffed."

"Why would I do that? A good cleaner is hard to find. She does a good job, doesn't she?"

Oh yeah. She did a great job—using magic, while she lay on the sofa eating my chocolates and drinking my wine.

"How much more is she going to charge?"

"Another fiver a week."

I was obviously in the wrong business.

Chapter 10

"Foxtrot or quickstep?" Jack said when I came down to breakfast.

"What are you talking about?"

"Which dance do you think we should practise tonight?"

"I think I need breakfast." I opened the fridge. "Where are the sausages?"

"I threw them out."

"You did what? Why would you do that?"

"They were past their 'best before' date?"

"Had they started to smell?"

"No, but—"

"Don't you know that the 'best before' date is just a cunning plan by the food industry to get you to buy more?"

"And there was I thinking it was to prevent food poisoning."

"You can be so naïve sometimes."

"Anyway, about the dancing?"

"I can't think about that right now. I'm still half-asleep."

"Okay, I'll make a decision. We'll start with the quickstep."

"Great. Can't wait."

"You should tell Kathy your good news."

"Which bit? There's so much of it."

"About the tickets, of course."

I'd had a horrible nightmare about being crushed in the mosh pit at the 'We' concert.

"Aren't we all a bit old to be in the standing area?"

"Of course not. It's the best place to see a gig. You're

almost on stage with the band."

"I'd hardly call 'We' a band. It's just Brenda."

"Even so. You can't beat the atmosphere of the mosh pit. Go on. Give Kathy a call."

"I'll do it later. I have some sausages to rescue from the bin first."

**

As soon as I walked out of the front door, Blake came rushing across the road.

"Jill! Can I have a word?"

"What's up?"

"Can we go inside?"

"Sure." Jack had already left for work, so I led the way back into the house. "What's wrong, Blake?"

"I'm being blackmailed."

"Who by? What about?"

"Someone is threatening to give me up to the rogue retrievers. Somehow, they've found out that I've told Jen I'm a wizard."

"Do you have any idea who could be behind it?"

"None."

"What do they want?"

He pulled a crumpled piece of paper out of his jacket pocket. "Look."

I read the note. In classic blackmail style, it had been put together from letters cut from a newspaper.

"Five thousand pounds?"

"I don't have that kind of money to spare. I don't know what to do."

"It says you have a week to come up with the money."

"It might as well be a year. I still wouldn't be able to find that kind of cash, and even if I could, what's to stop them from coming back for more? If they inform on me, that will be it for us. The rogue retrievers will haul me back to Candlefield, and Jen will be all alone. I'm really worried, Jill."

"Does anyone apart from me know that you've told Jen you're a wizard?"

"Not a soul."

"Are you absolutely sure? What about the sups you work with? Or your relatives?"

"I haven't told anyone else. I promise."

"It must have come from Jen. You know what she's like with secrets."

"Jen promised she wouldn't say anything to anyone else."

"It could have come from the blog."

"She's closed that down."

"Maybe someone had already worked out who she was before she took the blog down?"

"I guess that's possible." He bowed his head. "It looks like I'm done for."

"Don't give up yet. Let me see what I can find out."

"I can't afford to pay you."

"Don't worry about that. You're a neighbour, so you get the one hundred per cent discounted rate."

"Thanks, Jill. You're an angel."

***

Mrs V and Jules were much more chipper.
"Isn't it meant to be your day off, Jules?"

"Yes. I just popped in for a few minutes. Annabel and I wanted to talk to you about something."

"If it's about the hat and the tea cosy, I've already apologised for that."

"It isn't that," Mrs V said. "We realise that wasn't your fault."

"I'm glad I'm off the hook. What did you want to talk to me about, then?"

"The two of us spend a lot of time in this office," Mrs V said. "And to be perfectly honest, it's rather drab and depressing."

"How do you mean?"

"Just look around, Jill. The last time this room saw a lick of paint, your father was still alive."

She was right. The room was long overdue for a facelift—my office too.

"Can we get the decorators in, Jill?" Jules said.

"Provided it doesn't cost too much. I'm not sure what I'll do with Winky while they're painting my office, though."

"Chuck him out onto the street for a few days," Mrs V suggested. "He'll survive."

"I can't do that. He hasn't forgiven me for Bob yet."

"Who's Bob?" Jules said.

"Bob? He—err—was—err—Winky's favourite toy: A toy mouse."

"I thought that stupid cat was scared of mice?" Mrs V said.

"So did I. That's why I threw it out, but it turns out that he was actually Winky's favourite toy."

"How do you know that it was his favourite toy?" Jules asked way too many questions.

"I'm his owner. I can sense these things."

"Anyway," Mrs V said. "About the decorator. I thought we could have a nice shade of green in here."

"Green?" Jules looked horrified. "Green is boring. We should have red and pink."

Now it was Mrs V's turn to look horrified. "If you think I'm going to work in an office painted red, you have another think coming, young lady."

"Whoa, you two!" I interrupted. "When you've agreed on a colour scheme, let me know."

"I heard your lies." Winky was waiting for me just inside my office. "Why didn't you tell them the truth about Bob?"

"I didn't think you'd want them to know that you had a spider as a best friend."

"*Used to have*, don't you mean? You didn't tell them because you're ashamed that you murdered my only friend."

"That's a bit strong. I'd hardly call it murder. It was a tragic accident."

"I'm not sure I'll ever be able to forgive you."

"What about some nice salmon?"

"Red, not pink?"

"Obviously."

"And a double helping?"

"Of course."

I'd have to hope that it would take Mrs V and Jules some time to agree on a colour scheme. With all the money I was spending on salmon, I wasn't sure I'd have any left to get the office redecorated.

***

I was at the radio station to speak to Lee Sparks' producer, Dale Royal. For some reason, I'd always pictured the radio station as being based in ultra-modern premises. In fact, it was located in a small unit on an industrial estate.

"Morning." The receptionist was Bubbly. Not in the joyful sense of the word—far from it—she was actually a bit miserable. Her name was Susie Bubbly.

"That's an unusual name," I commented.

"Susie? I know. I hate it. I don't know why my parents couldn't have given me a sensible name like Pumpkin. My best friend is called Pumpkin. I think it's the best name in the world."

Huh? "I meant your last name: Bubbly. I've never come across that before, but then I guess a lot of people must tell you that?"

"No, you're the first. Is there something I can do for you?"

"I have an appointment with Dale Royal. I'm Jill Gooder."

"Gooder? And you think Bubbly is a strange name?"

Dale Royal had hiccups.

"Hi. I'm *hiccup* Dale."

"Jill Gooder. Thanks for seeing me."

"Would you like to come through *hiccup* to the studio?"

"Sure."

He led the way to a small studio, which overlooked a larger room from which the DJs broadcast their shows.

"Is that where Lee Sparks was murdered?"

"Yes *hiccup*. Right there in that *hiccup* chair."

"Would you like to go and get a drink?"

"Sorry?"

"For your hiccups."

"It won't do any good. I've had them all day. I've tried absolutely — "

"Boo!" I shouted at him, and he almost fell off his seat.

"Why did you do that?"

"Have they gone? Your hiccups?"

He waited for a few moments. "I think so. Thanks."

"I understand you were producing the show when Lee Sparks died."

"Yes. I produced all of his shows."

"And yet, you didn't see anything?"

"He'd sent me down the road for coffee."

"Was that usual? Aren't you supposed to stay in here while the show is on air?"

"Lee treated me like his own personal slave. I was no more than a gopher to him."

"I take it you weren't a fan?"

"He thought he was something special. That he knew it all."

"Why did you put up with it?"

"What choice did I have? Lee was the station's star. Producers are ten a penny. I can't afford to lose this job; I have a family to feed."

"Did he seem okay when you left to fetch the coffee?"

"Yeah. He was his usual obnoxious self."

"And you didn't see anyone hanging around the studio when you went out?"

"No. Like I told the police. I didn't see anyone either on

my way out or when I came back."

"Can you describe what you found when you got back?"

"I heard a scream when I was on my way down the corridor. When I walked in, Kylie had her back up against this glass."

"What was she doing?"

"Nothing. She was hysterical."

"This is very important. Did you see Kylie touch the knife?"

"No. Like I said, she'd moved away from Lee, and was up against the glass."

"Had Lee seemed okay that day?"

"He was just the same as always."

"Do you know if he met with anyone else earlier?"

"Not that I saw, but then I only arrived a short time before the show was due to go on air. I could take a look at his calendar, if you like? It's on the computer."

"You have his password?"

"He thought it was part of my job to update his calendar." Royal logged onto the computer, which was on the table behind him.

"There. It looks like he had a couple of meetings in the morning before his show."

The first entry was for a meeting at Sounds coffee shop at ten o'clock with Raymond Conway, Lee Sparks' ex-manager. The second meeting was with Mike Spins, the DJ that Sparks had replaced on the drivetime show.

I would need to speak to those two gentlemen, but first, I wanted another word with Pumpkin wannabe, Susie Bubbly.

"Hi. It's me again."

Judging by the blank expression on her face, she'd already forgotten who I was. This woman obviously had the memory of a goldfish.

"I was here a few minutes ago. I've been with Dale Royal."

"Oh, yeah. I remember."

"Are there any other entrances to the radio station?"

"No. Just this one."

"And is reception always manned?"

"Yeah. Two of us take it in turns to work the day shift; one of the security men is here during the night."

"Dale Royal said it would be okay for me to look at the CCTV coverage for the day that Lee Sparks was murdered," I lied.

"I don't know how to work it."

"That's okay, I do. If you could just point me to the office where it's kept?"

"It's in the security office, down that corridor, but you'll have to clear it with Bert."

"Who's Bert?"

"He's the security man who's in charge of the CCTV. He's usually in that office."

"Okay, thanks."

I knew as soon as I saw Bert that I wasn't going to get any joy out of him. He had 'job's worth' written all over his smug face. I could have wasted thirty minutes using all my powers of persuasion, and my feminine wiles, but I couldn't be bothered.

I used the 'sleep' spell instead.

With Bert snoozing in his chair, I viewed the CCTV coverage of that fateful day, starting from a point a couple of hours before Lee Sparks' show went on air. Mike Spins was the first person to appear—he was probably on his way to his meeting with Lee Sparks. Fifteen minutes later, Sparks showed up. During the next hour, three other people came into the building, but they didn't go any further than the reception area. Next to enter was Dale Royal, a few minutes ahead of the show he was about to produce. Shortly after that, Mike Spins left the building. Shortly after the time-stamp showed it was time for the drivetime show to begin, Dale Royal reappeared. He was headed out of the building—presumably on his way to Sounds, to get coffee for Sparks. Kylie Jay arrived next. Was that the face of a woman hellbent on murdering her boyfriend? She certainly didn't look very happy. A few minutes later, Dale Royal returned—coffee in hand.

I woke Bert, and cast the 'forget' spell on him before making my way out of the radio station. The CCTV had done no more than confirm what I already knew—it had revealed nothing unexpected.

***

Bertie Myflowers lived in an apartment block, which was close to the market square in GT.

"It's true, then?" Myflowers was staring at me. "Constance Bowler told me that you were a sup, but I thought she was pulling my leg. I didn't think it was possible for you lot to visit Ghost Town."

"Neither did I, but here I am. Constance tells me you've had some dealings with the ghost traffickers?"

"That's right. Come in." He led the way into a lovely little sitting room. For a ghost, Bertie Myflowers certainly had an eye for interior design.

"Lovely place you have here, Mr Myflowers."

"Call me Bertie, please. I can't take the credit for any of this. It's all the work of my sister, Gertie."

"Bertie and Gertie?"

"I'm afraid so. My mother thought it was cute for us to have rhyming names."

"Could you talk me through your experience with the traffickers?"

"Sure. I've wanted to go back to the human world ever since — err — well — ever since I left it. The problem is that all my relatives are over here."

"Including your sister?"

"She electrocuted herself two years before I passed over."

"What about friends?"

"Not really. I always kept myself to myself. Of course, if I'd realised that having friends would make the difference between being able to get back to the human world, or staying here, I'd have made more of an effort. When I saw an ad for Ghost Placements, I thought I'd found the answer to my prayers."

"If I understand correctly, they promise to find a human host for you?"

"That's right. It sounded perfect."

"What went wrong?"

"As soon as I arrived at their offices, I got bad vibes."

"Why?"

"I can't explain it. There was just something that didn't feel right."

"Were there any other customers there on the day you went?"

"There were eight of us altogether. Everyone else

seemed excited to get on with it, but something held me back. I asked a few questions, but never got a straight answer."

"What kind of questions?"

"When I asked where the human hosts were located, they said they had lots on their books, but they wouldn't know which one we'd be going to until they'd had time to find the optimum match."

"Anything else?"

"I asked if we'd be able to come back to GT whenever we wanted."

"What did they say?"

"They didn't give me a proper answer; they just skirted around my question. That's when I decided it wasn't for me."

"Did you have any problem getting away?"

"Not really. I just pretended I didn't have the cash. After that, they weren't interested in me. I still feel guilty because I went there with a work colleague, Andy Toeloop. I tried to persuade him to leave with me, but he was determined to go through with it."

"Have you seen anything of him since then?"

"No one has."

Chapter 11

This time I was determined to take a good look around the market in GT. It was extremely busy, and I had to squeeze my way through the crowds. It didn't help that everywhere I went, people stopped and stared at me. A sup in GT was still a newsworthy event, unfortunately. The sooner that situation changed, the happier I'd be.

"Jill! Over here!"

I could hear my mother's voice, but I couldn't see her through the crowd.

"Mum?"

"Can you meet us over by the statues, Jill?"

"Okay. Will do."

I'd noticed the statues on my way into the market. When I reached them, my mother and Alberto were both straining their necks to try to see me.

"I'm here."

"Jill." Mum gave me a hug. "It so great that you're able to visit GT now, isn't it Alberto?"

"It certainly is." He flashed a huge smile.

"Are you two out shopping for anything in particular?"

"Just a garden gnome," my mother said.

"Very funny. What are you really looking for?"

"A garden gnome. Alberto collects them, don't you?"

His smile had disappeared. "Don't you like garden gnomes, Jill?"

"Gnomes? I love them. I've been telling Jack that we should get one for ages now."

"If you need any advice, I'll be pleased to help."

"That's very kind, thanks." I figured it might be best to get off the subject of garden gnomes. "What's with these statues?"

"How do you mean?" My mother glanced up at them.

"They're a little unusual, aren't they?"

"In what way?"

"Well, it's not every day you see statues of vegetables with arms and legs. Don't you think they're a little creepy?"

"We like them, don't we, Alberto? We often sit here to have our lunch."

"Right." Just me, then.

"What brings you over here today?" said my mother, the creepy-statue enthusiast.

"I'm working on a case with Constance Bowler."

"Don't you think you already have enough on your plate, solving cases in Washbridge and Candlefield? You'll wear yourself out."

"I'm fine, Mum. There's nothing for you to worry about, honestly."

"Are you eating properly? You look as though you've lost weight."

"I'm eating just fine, or at least I would be if Jack didn't keep throwing out the sausages."

"Sorry?"

"Nothing. I'm fine, honestly."

"You must come to dinner with us this Sunday, mustn't she, Alberto?"

"Definitely." His smile was back. "You can experience my special mashed potatoes. They're awfully good, although I do say so myself."

"I'd love to, but—" I stopped myself just in time. If I told my mother that I was having Sunday lunch with my father and Blodwyn, she'd go ballistic. "I—err—I'd love to."

"Great. That's settled then. We'll see you on Sunday."

Oh bum! What had I just done?

**

I'd agreed to meet Aunt Lucy later, to help her choose an outfit. I was worried because I had no idea what people would wear at a grim reaper dinner and dance. But I did know someone who would. I made a call, and to my delight they agreed to help.

I'd no sooner finished on that call than my phone rang. It was Kathy.

"You and your brilliant ideas, Jill."

"Sorry? What did I do this time?"

"*You should go on strike*, she says. *That will show Grandma*, she says."

"I stand by what I said. You can't just let her walk all over you."

"That's all well and good, but she's sacked us both, and taken on temporary staff. Thanks to you, I no longer have a job."

"She can't do that! It must be against the law."

"Do you think your grandmother cares about that?"

"Don't worry. I'll get it sorted."

"And how do you intend to do that?"

"I'll go down to Ever, and talk to Grandma."

"When has she ever listened to a single word you say?"

"It'll be okay, Kathy. I promise."

"It had better be. Oh, and by the way, I had a strange phone call from a man, asking if I wanted bagpipe lessons. He said you gave him my number."

"What? He was probably drunk or crazy."

"So, you don't know anything about it?"

"Not a thing. I'd better get going. Bye."

This was all my own stupid fault. I should have kept my nose out of Kathy's grievances with Grandma. What had I been thinking? Somehow, I had to make this right.

***

Nothing could have prepared me for the scene which greeted me at Ever. The place was full to bursting; the queue at the counter snaked all around the shop. A number of disgruntled customers were complaining loudly.

"What do you expect me to do about it?" the young woman behind the counter shrugged. She had spiked black and purple hair, a lip piercing, and a mouthful of gum.

"I paid for multi-coloured wool, and it isn't working!" the middle-aged woman at the counter was red in the face. "I expect you to sort it out."

Just then, there was a loud crash. I followed the noise into the tea room.

"Look what you've done!" An irate middle-aged woman was wiping her legs.

"Chill! It was an accident." A young woman, covered in tattoos, bent down and began to pick up the pieces of the cups she'd dropped onto the floor. Tea and coffee had splashed everywhere.

Where was Grandma? Did she have any idea what was going on? I tried her office, but it was empty, so I hurried up to the roof terrace. It was deserted except for one sunlounger at the far side of the roof. Lying there, in her bathing costume and sunglasses, was the woman herself.

"Grandma!"

She didn't react.

"Grandma!" I yelled louder.

Still no reaction, but now I could see why. She had earphones in.

"Grandma!" I shook her arm.

"Do you mind?" She jumped up, and took out the earphones.

"Why are you hiding away up here?"

"I'm not hiding; I'm relaxing. At least, I was trying to until you interrupted me. It's the least I deserve after having to put up with all the aggravation caused by your militant sister and her buddy."

"Who are those two working in the shop?"

"Those are the temporary replacements. And it's no good begging me to give your sister her job back. She's burned her boats."

"Have you actually been down into the shop since the temps started?"

"No, why would I? I've already told you that I need to recharge my batteries after the upset caused by your wayward sibling."

"I think you might want to take a look down there."

"Why? What's going on?"

I started towards the stairs. "I wouldn't want to spoil the surprise."

***

Aunt Lucy was waiting for me outside Wendy's

Fashions, as arranged.

"Sorry I'm late," I said. "I had to go to Ever."

"More problems?"

"Yes, but not for me this time."

"I'm still not sure what I'm looking for, Jill. Have you had any bright ideas?"

"As it happens, I've had a brilliant idea, but I'm not too sure how you're going to feel about it."

"I'm willing to listen to any advice. I just don't want to make a colossal fool of myself at this dinner and dance."

"I'm pleased to hear you say that because I've asked someone to join us." I checked the time. "In fact, she should be here any moment now."

"Who?" Aunt Lucy had no sooner said the word than my 'secret weapon' arrived.

"Thanks for coming, Monica," I said.

"My pleasure. I'm only too pleased to help." She turned to Aunt Lucy. "That's always provided that you'd like my input?"

"I—err—?" Aunt Lucy looked and sounded stunned.

"Monica has been to the grim reaper dance before," I said. "She knows much better than I do what will be appropriate."

"That makes sense, I guess." Aunt Lucy turned to Monica. "Thank you. I'd appreciate your help."

I sighed with relief. "I'm going to leave you two to it."

Aunt Lucy looked horrified. I knew she would have preferred me to stay, but she wasn't about to say anything in front of Monica. So far, my plan was going well. Hopefully, they wouldn't end up at each other's throats.

While in Candlefield, I decided to take a muffin break in

Cuppy C. The tea-room was practically empty; the Alan and William fangirls had obviously moved on. It wasn't quiet though because there was a loud banging noise coming from somewhere out back.

"Hi, Jill. I thought you were meant to be shopping with Mum?" Pearl was by herself behind the counter.

"I've arranged for someone much more knowledgeable to stand in for me."

"Who?"

"Monica."

"Mum hates Monica."

"Hopefully, this will change that."

"Either that or they'll end up murdering one another." Pearl grinned. "And then both of them will murder you."

"In that case, you'd better serve a blueberry muffin to the condemned woman."

"What are you doing here?" Amber had come through from the cake shop.

"She's left Mum shopping with Monica," Pearl said, as she handed me a muffin.

"You're so dead." Amber grinned. "Haven't you heard the way Mum talks about Monica? She hates her."

"You underestimate my skills of diplomacy. Before the day is out, they'll be besties." I took a bite of muffin. "What's that terrible racket coming from out back?"

"Before we tell you." Pearl handed me a latte. "Would you agree that the art exhibition was a success?"

"I suppose so."

"Why so begrudging?" Amber said. "You saw how many people attended."

"And, they were the right sort of people," Pearl added.

"The *right sort*? You two are such snobs. But, yes, I have

to admit the art exhibition went better than I could ever have imagined. What does that have to do with the noise coming from out back?"

"What you can hear is the next exciting phase in the evolution of Cuppy C."

"The evolution? Have you been practising that speech?"

"Look, Jill," Amber said. "We understand that you're rather stuck in your ways when it comes to business."

"What do you mean by that?"

"You just keep on with the same old, same old. When was the last time you tried to improve your business? Where are the new initiatives? The new innovations?"

"I—err—I'm always innovating."

"Name one example." Pearl pressed me.

"Okay. I—err—I had some new business cards printed only last week. They're embossed. Would you like to see one?"

"Is that your idea of innovative?" It was Amber's turn to put the boot in.

"There are other examples too, but I'm not at liberty to discuss them. The very nature of my business means those things have to be kept confidential."

"You're so full of it, Jill." Pearl laughed.

"You two still haven't told me what's going on out back." The banging was getting louder.

"We're going to open a drive-thru," Pearl said, proudly.

"A what? Where? How?"

"Where do you think?" Amber looked at me as though I was a simpleton. "Around the back of course. The noise you can hear is someone installing a serving hatch."

"Hold on a minute. How can you have a drive-thru around the back? There isn't a road back there."

"Have you forgotten about the alleyway?" Pearl said.

"It's very narrow."

"It's wide enough," Amber insisted. "Don't you think we would have checked?"

"Sorry. Well, I guess it could work."

"Your enthusiasm is overwhelming as always. Drive-thrus are all the rage now. People are so busy that they often don't have time to visit a tea room. This way, they can enjoy all that Cuppy C has to offer, to-go."

"It's definitely an improvement on the delivery service idea," I conceded. "Whatever did happen to those scooters?"

Chapter 12

"Aren't you excited?" Jack asked.

It was Saturday—the day of SupsCon, and despite my valiant efforts, I'd been unable to talk him out of it.

"I can barely control my excitement."

"Me neither."

Sarcasm? It was totally lost on the man.

"Do you think we should put on our costumes here at home?" He was examining his plastic fangs.

"No, of course not. No one in their right mind would drive one hundred miles dressed as a vampire. Everyone will get changed there."

"I guess you're right. What time is it? We don't want to be late."

"Fat chance of that after you set the alarm an hour earlier than we needed to get up." I yawned.

"Mum called last night, to check that everything was okay for Monday. I told her that we were looking forward to seeing her."

"Did she say anything about me?"

"Such as?"

"Such as: *Have you dumped that waste of space yet?*"

"I'm not going to dignify that stupidity with an answer."

It was time to leave. I'd seriously considered feigning a last-minute tummy bug, but I knew there was zero chance that Jack would have bought it.

"Oh? Tony looked us up and down. Both he and Clare were wearing their costumes. "We should have mentioned that it's best to change beforehand. Security down there is pretty lax, and there are no lockers. Most people travel there in costume."

"We didn't realise," Jack said. "We'll go and change,"

Once we were back inside the house, he gave me a look.

"What? How was I supposed to know that we were meant to put our costumes on?"

"I didn't say a word."

"You didn't need to. You were giving me *the look*."

Oh boy! The day was getting off to a great start.

Resplendent in our vampire costumes, we joined Tony and Clare in the car. Jack sat up front, and I slid alongside Clare in the back.

"I love your costume." Clare looked me up and down with the experienced eye of a cosplay veteran. "What about your fangs?"

"I thought I'd put those in when we get there."

"I have mine in." Jack turned around, and flashed the plastic canines.

"You look great, Jack," Clare said.

"And you make a fantastic witch, doesn't she, Jill?"

"Very authentic," I agreed, half-heartedly.

"Jill wanted to go as a witch," Jack said. "I told her she wasn't really witch material."

Not witch material? Cheek! The temptation to demonstrate my witchy skills had never been so great.

When we pulled up at the toll booth, I spotted Mr Ivers, ducking out of sight.

"There's no one to collect the money." Tony looked confused. So did Jack and Clare. I'd been the only one to spot Mr Ivers' disappearing act.

"I'll sort this." I climbed out of the car, and walked over to the booth. "Mr Ivers?" I knocked on the glass. "It's okay, you can come out. It's me, Jill."

Slowly, and very nervously, he raised his head. "I thought I was under attack from paranormal creatures."

"Sorry to scare you. We're just on our way to a cosplay thingy."

"What's cosplay?"

"It's where grown people play at dressing up," I said in a hushed voice so as not to upset the neighbours.

After Mr Ivers had taken the cash, I climbed back into the car, and we were on our way again.

Have you ever sat in a car dressed as a vampire? If you have, then you will know that you attract some strange looks. And none stranger than from my old friend, Leo Riley. We were on our way through Washbridge when we pulled up at a set of traffic lights. And who should pull up in the lane next to us? You guessed it. My favourite detective. The look on his face was priceless.

Two hours later, we arrived at SupsCon. After parking the car, we joined the queue that snaked around the forecourt in front of the conference centre. I had no idea that cosplay was so popular. Or why.

"Put your fangs in," Jack whispered.

"Okay." I shoved the stupid things into my mouth. "It's going to take ages just to get inside."

"I can't tell what you're saying."

"That's because I've got these stupid things in my mouth."

"What did you say?"

I pulled the fangs out. "I said it's going to take ages just to get inside."

"It'll be worth the wait, though. There are some great costumes, aren't there?"

He was right; there were some fabulous costumes. But it was something else that had caught my attention. At least one-third of the people in the queue were sups! I couldn't get my head around it. I was there because I'd practically been press-ganged into it, but why did all the other sups want to go to a cosplay event—just to dress as sups? It made no sense.

Jack, Tony and Clare were deep in conversation, as we made our way slowly towards the entrance. While they were distracted, I managed to grab a word with a couple of werewolves who were dressed as—wait for it—that's right—werewolves!

"Hey, guys. What's the deal?"

"How do you mean?"

"Why would you come here and *pretend* to be a werewolf, when you really are—"

"Shush!" They both looked around. "Someone might hear."

"Sorry," I whispered. "I just don't get why you'd want to do it."

"We normally don't get the chance to be ourselves in the human world because we run the risk of being arrested by the rogue retrievers. But here, we can be ourselves for a few hours. It's very liberating."

"I hadn't considered that."

"Can I ask you something?" the taller of the two said.

"Sure."

"Why would a witch want to come dressed as a vampire?"

"Because, according to my human partner, I'd make a terrible witch."

That gave them both a good laugh.

When we eventually made it inside, I immediately wished we hadn't bothered. The venue was packed to bursting, and if there was aircon in there, it wasn't very effective. I was sweating buckets.

What? Okay then. I was perspiring buckets. Happy now?

I followed the other three as we made our way from one stand to another. Tony and Clare seemed to have money to burn, as they bought all manner of memorabilia.

"We should get those." Jack pointed to ceramic models of Vamp and Champ.

"Why?"

"As a reminder of today."

Why would anyone want to be reminded of this travesty?

"They're expensive."

"Not really."

"Where would we put them?"

"In the lounge."

"Where people can see them?"

"Why not?"

There was no reasoning with him.

"We should all enter this!" Tony was holding up a flyer.

"What is it?" Jack was Mr Keen, as always.

"It's a competition to choose the best costume — there's a prize for each different category of supernatural creature."

"We're in," Jack announced.

We?

"Great." Tony nodded. I'll put all four of our names forward. The entrance fee is ten pounds."

"For the four of us?" I said, more in hope than expectation.

"Each."

Lunch comprised an over-priced sandwich, and lukewarm tea in a paper cup.

"What do you think of SupsCon, so far?" Tony asked.

"It's great fun." Jack gushed.

"Jill?" Tony turned to me.

"Err—yeah—great—err—fun."

"How does the competition work?" Jack asked.

"It's pretty straightforward. Everyone has to report to the smaller hall next door. There'll be a section for witches and wizards, another for vampires, another for werewolves etc. The judges walk around and mark each of the competitors, and then they announce the winners. It's just a bit of fun really."

"I think we should be in with a good chance," Jack said. Always the competitor.

"Where's the nearest loo?" I asked.

Clare pointed the way. "Do you want me to go with you?"

"No, it's okay."

I've never understood why some women feel the need to go to the ladies' room in pairs. And besides, I didn't actually need to go. I just wanted to get out of there for some fresh air.

The doorman stamped the back of my hand on my way out. In the forecourt, I sat down on the steps—thankful to get out of that clammy atmosphere.

"You look like you're enjoying this about as much as I am." A female vampire, dressed in a witch's outfit, was standing on the step below mine. "Do you mind if I join you?"

"Help yourself."

"I'm Kirsty."

"Jill."

"Let me guess. Your guy told you that you wouldn't make a good witch?" she said.

"Got it in one. Same for you?"

"Yep. Apparently, I'd be an awful vampire." She grinned and flashed her real fangs. "I love Bill, that's my guy, to bits. But seriously, humans can be super stupid sometimes."

"I'll drink to that."

Kirsty and I spent the next twenty minutes bemoaning our lot, but then we both had to get back inside for the competition.

"Good luck," she said, and then disappeared into the crowd.

"Where have you been?" Jack looked flustered. "I didn't think you were going to make it. It's almost time for the competition."

"There was a queue." I kept my hand behind my back in case he noticed the stamp.

The four of us filed through to the smaller hall. Tony and Clare made their way to the witch and wizard section while Jack and I headed for the vampire section.

"Have you got your fangs in?" Jack stared at my mouth.

"I can't talk with them in."

"We have no chance of winning if you don't wear

them."

"Okay." I shoved them into my mouth.

The competition was for couples, so Jack and I had to stick close to one another while the two judges passed among us.

"Jill, flash your fangs when the judges are nearby." Jack was taking this way too seriously.

After just under an hour, an announcement came over the loudspeaker: *All competitors should now leave their section, and make their way in front of the main stage. The winners will be announced in a few minutes.*

Jack was getting more and more excited, as the head judge announced the various winners. When it came to the witch and wizard category, Tony and Clare didn't place in the top three, but they seemed to take it all in good part.

"And now, we come to the vampire category. In third place, we have Angela and Morgan Fairside."

There was a smattering of polite applause as they made their way on stage to collect the world's smallest trophy.

"In second place, we have Christine and Christopher Chrisling."

Seriously?

"And in first place –" He paused for dramatic effect. I just wanted him to hurry up and get it over with, so we could go home. *"Give it up for Jill Gooder and Jack Maxwell."*

What the – ?

"Come on!" Jack grabbed my arm, and dragged me on stage to collect our trophy, which was only marginally bigger than those for second and third places.

"Well done, you two!" Clare greeted us when we re-joined them.

"Yeah! Well done!" Tony was almost as pleased as if he'd won.

As we made our way out of the building, I heard several vampires moaning, under their breath. They were complaining about the outrage of a witch and a human placing above 'the real thing'. To be fair, they had a point.

When we finally got back home, I couldn't wait to get into the house, so I could take off the stupid vampire costume.

"Tony, Clare, why don't you come inside for a nightcap?" Jack said.

"Are you sure?" Clare must have seen my expression. "Jill looks tired."

"She's okay, aren't you?" Jack turned to me.

"Sure. I'm fine. Come on in."

Jack poured a glass of wine for everyone.

"I'll go and get changed." I started for the door.

"Wait." Jack took hold of my arm. "We need a photo first."

"Great idea." Tony took out his phone. "You and Jill stand over there, and hold the trophy between you."

It was futile to argue, so I did as he said.

"Okay! Say fangs!"

Chapter 13

The tiny cosplay trophy now had pride of place on our mantelpiece. I'd suggested putting (hiding) it in the spare bedroom, but Jack wouldn't hear of it. That man just loved his trophies.

Speaking of which, he'd left home at the crack of dawn to take part in an all-day ten-pin bowling competition. I thought he'd want me to go along and support him, but he said that I'd just be a distraction. I wasn't sure if that was a compliment or not.

Probably not.

It was just as well he didn't want me there because I already had a full day ahead of me. Like an idiot, I'd agreed to have Sunday lunch at my mother's house, and then another one at my father's. If I'd had any sense, I would have told my mother that I already had something arranged, but I'd been worried about how she might react. Fortunately, I had a little time between the two meals. I was due at my mother's house at midday, and at my father's at two. If I restricted how much I ate during the first lunch, I should still be able to eat at least some of the second one.

What is it they say about the best laid plans?

When I magicked myself to GT, I had to make sure that I landed right outside my mother's house. If my father or Blodwyn saw me, I would have some explaining to do.

"You're a little early." My mother gave me a hug. "Lunch will be another ten minutes."

"Is it okay if I just have a small portion?"

"Why ever would you want a small portion? Look at

yourself. You're all skin and bone."

If my mother honestly thought I was 'all skin and bone', she needed to get her eyes checked. If anything, I was a little heavier than I would have liked, but I put that down to Jack's cooking.

"My tummy has been a little iffy. I don't want to overdo it."

"Okay, a small portion it is."

"Jill!" Alberto joined us. "Why don't I show you my garden gnomes while we're waiting?"

"Yeah." My mother nodded. "He has an impressive collection."

"Sure, why not?" And there was I thinking that nothing could possibly top the excitement of the cosplay convention.

Alberto led the way through the house, out of the French doors, and into the beautifully-maintained garden.

"What a lot of gnomes. How long have you been collecting them?"

"Ever since I arrived in GT. They all have names."

Oh boy!

"Your mother named that one 'Jill'. She thought it looked like you."

"The one with the big nose?"

"It has such a lovely smile, don't you think?"

"My nose isn't *that* big."

If this was my mother's idea of a small portion, I was glad she hadn't given me a large one.

"Gravy, Jill?" Alberto offered.

"Not for me, thanks."

The meal looked and smelled delicious, and under

different circumstances, I would probably have polished it off, but I had to leave room for lunch mark-two. My main concern was the two enormous Yorkshire puddings.

"That's pretty." I pointed to the clock on the far wall. While my mother and Alberto were distracted, I slipped the two Yorkshire puddings into my bag.

"The clock?" My mother turned back to me.

"Yes. I really like the—err—minute hand. The hour hand is very nice too."

I ignored their puzzled looks.

"Do you have to leave so soon?" My mother was clearing the table. "Your lunch has barely had time to settle. You're welcome to stay as long as you like."

"I haven't shown you all of my gnomes yet," Alberto said.

"I'd love to stay longer, but I promised to meet up with Mad while I'm here. Maybe next time."

I hoped they would just see me to the door, but they came outside, so I had to walk up the street, in the opposite direction to my father's house. When they finally went back inside, I turned around and raced back down the street.

"Jill?" My father greeted me. "You look exhausted. Are you okay?"

"Fine, thanks."

"Hello, Jill." Blodwyn joined us.

"Thanks for inviting me, Blodwyn."

"It's our pleasure."

"Do you think I could just have a small serving?"

"Small?" My father jumped in. "There are no small servings in this house, are there, Blod?"

"It's just that my tummy has been a little iffy, and I don't want to overdo it."

"Oh dear. I won't give you too much in that case," Blodwyn said. "Let me take your coat."

As I put my bag down, it fell over, and the two Yorkshire puddings rolled out onto the floor. My father and Blodwyn exchanged a puzzled glance.

"Err—I thought I—err better bring my own Yorkshire puddings, just in case you didn't make any. I can't eat a Sunday lunch without a Yorkshire pudding."

"That's very thoughtful of you." Blodwyn was no doubt trying to humour the crazy woman. "It's okay, though, because I have made Yorkshire puddings."

"I guess I'll take these back for Jack, then."

More puzzled expressions ensued.

"Or I could just throw them in the bin."

This was getting off to such an auspicious start.

"Would you like to meet the dogs while Blodwyn puts the finishing touches to lunch?" my father asked.

"I didn't realise you had any."

"They were Blodwyn's originally. Come and meet them."

As soon as we stepped out into the back garden, the two dogs came charging over. Fortunately, the corgis weren't big enough to do any real harm when they jumped up at me.

"That's Daff, and this one is Dill."

"Oh? They're sweet."

"Sweet, but very crafty. We have to leave them in the garden while we eat our meals, otherwise they'd be begging for food all the time."

"Lunch is served!" Blodwyn called through the

window.

It seemed that she shared my mother's inability to understand the meaning of the word 'small' because my plate was overflowing.

"Are those Yorkshire puddings alright for you, Jill?"

"Lovely, thanks."

"I gave you three, seeing as how you're so fond of them."

"Great."

Ten minutes later, and I'd barely managed to eat any of the meal. My stomach already felt as though it was about to burst, but I wasn't too worried because I had a plan.

"Would you mind if I opened this window?" I said. "I'm a little warm."

"Of course."

Part one of the plan executed.

"That's pretty." I pointed.

As my father and Blodwyn followed my gaze, I grabbed the meat from my plate, and threw it out of the window.

"Do you mean the clock?" Blodwyn wore the same puzzled expression that I was growing accustomed to seeing.

"Yes. I like the font they've used for the numbers."

"Whatever is wrong with those two?" My father was referring to the barking coming from the back garden.

Blodwyn stood up. "Daff! Dill! Be quiet!"

If she saw the meat, I'd have a lot of explaining to do.

"What's wrong with them?" my father asked.

"They're just acting crazy as usual." She re-joined us at the table.

Phew! It seemed like I'd got away with it.

"Would you like pudding?" Blodwyn asked, when I finally admitted defeat with what was left of the main course.

"Not for me, thanks. I couldn't eat another mouthful. That was a lovely meal."

After they'd cleared the table, we all retired to the lounge.

"How did all this come about?" My father was in a rocking chair. "Your being able to travel to GT?"

"The original idea came from the police authorities here in Ghost Town. They wanted a sup who would be capable of working between all three worlds."

"Can't Mad do that?"

"Yes, but Mad is a parahuman; she isn't a sup. She's a brilliant ghost hunter, but she doesn't have any magical powers, as such."

"What sort of things will you be working on?" Blodwyn was seated next to me on the sofa.

"Long term, I'm not sure, but I've just taken on my first case."

"Can you tell us anything about it?" My father stopped rocking just long enough to grab his cup of coffee.

"I don't see why not. There have been reports of ghost trafficking. Ghosts, who have no one in the human world to whom they can attach themselves, are being sold the promise of a human host. It's obviously some kind of scam because the people who have signed up have disappeared without a trace."

"That's terrible," Blodwyn said. "What are you going to do about it?"

"I'm not sure at the moment. I need to track what happens to those who sign up. I can't sign up myself because I'm not a ghost, obviously."

"I'll do it." My father volunteered.

"Thanks for the offer, but that wouldn't work. It has to be someone who doesn't have friends or relatives in the human world. These people can easily check that, and would know that you're a fraud."

"What about me?" Blodwyn said.

"No!" My father snapped. "It's too dangerous."

"Not if Jill has my back. I don't have any relatives or friends left in the human world, so I'd get through their checks without any problems. What do you think, Jill?"

"Dad's right. It could be dangerous."

"Someone has to do it, Josh, otherwise that horrible trade will continue."

"What would it involve, exactly?" My father still looked doubtful.

"I need someone to sign up for the Ghost Placement service so I can track them, and find out where they are being taken."

"How do you plan on doing the tracking?"

"They'll be wearing a tracking device."

"Won't they be checked for those?"

"Possibly, but we have some which are undetectable."

"I'm up for it," Blodwyn said.

"Are you positive that she'll be safe, Jill?" My father turned to me.

"Yes, I'll be with her every step of the way."

I was so stuffed that I practically waddled back up the road. When I was out of sight of the house, I made a call to Mad.

"Hey, Jill. How goes it?"

"Okay, apart from my stomach."

"Are you ill?"

"No. I've just eaten two Sunday lunches."

"Why two?"

"It's a long story. Look, the reason I called is to ask if you know much about tracking devices."

"Not much, why?"

"I've just promised someone that we have some which are undetectable, so I thought I'd better find out if that was true."

"I'm pretty sure they can all be detected in one way or another."

Oh bum!

***

When I arrived home, Jack was standing in the lounge. He was still wearing his (horrible) bowling shirt, and was holding the largest trophy I'd ever seen.

"Had a good day, sweetie?" he greeted me, as soon as I walked in.

"Not bad."

"I've had a *really* good day." He had a silly grin on his face.

"That's nice."

"Aren't you going to ask?"

"Ask what?"

"About the trophy?"

"Oh, right. I hadn't noticed that."

"I won."

"Congrats."

"I think I might have to move the cosplay trophy

upstairs, to make room for this one."

"You're not planning on keeping that monstrous thing in here, surely?"

"How else will anyone know I won?"

"Couldn't I just snap a photo of you holding it? We could stick that *somewhere*, instead."

"I suppose you're right. This is rather large."

"Step back so I can get you and that ginormous thing in the shot. Smile! Okay, now take it up to the spare bedroom."

He started for the door. "I'm starving. What's for dinner?"

Chapter 14

"I had no idea that cosplay could be so exciting." Jack was spreading jam onto his toast.

"What flavour is that?" I turned the jar around. "Rhubarb? Seriously?"

"Jack Corner put me onto it. It was on special offer."

"I'm not surprised. He probably can't give the stuff away."

"What's wrong with rhubarb?"

"What's right with it? We have plenty of strawberry or blackcurrant jam."

"You have no sense of adventure, Jill."

"I like my breakfasts to be traditional, and that means no rhubarb jam, thank you very much."

"Mmm!" He took a bite and nodded his approval.

"Freak!"

"I bet Mum will like it."

I'd been doing my best not to think about his mother's visit. "What time is she coming?"

"Her train gets in at about four o' clock. I'm going to get out of work early, to pick her up. You can come with me if you like?"

"I'd love to, but I'm going to be busy all day."

"Not to worry. She'll be here when you get home from work."

"Do you think she'll talk to me this time?"

"I hope you aren't going to keep this up. Mum doesn't have it in for you—it's all in your mind."

"Just because I'm paranoid doesn't mean that your mother doesn't hate me."

"We ought to do something special for dinner."

"Who is this 'we' you speak of? Have you managed to talk Brenda into coming around here to make dinner?"

"Very funny. I'll make dinner. You'll just have to keep Mum entertained."

"What do you suggest? Juggling? How about a puppet show?"

I watched through the window, as Jack left for work. Across the road, Blake was just setting off too. That reminded me — I still hadn't done anything yet about the blackmail threat he'd received. It occurred to me that perhaps he was over-reacting. Maybe the rogue retrievers would turn a blind eye, provided that the couple were not broadcasting their situation. It was still early, but I knew that Daze would already be up, so I gave her a call.

"Jill? What's wrong?"

"Nothing. I'm sorry for calling so early."

"That's okay. It's just that phone calls at this time of day are usually bad news."

"Can I ask you a hypothetical question?"

"Shoot."

"If a sup and a human were living together as man and wife, and somehow word got out about the sup, would it be curtains for them?"

"Are you and Jack planning on getting married?"

"What? No. I'm not talking about me and Jack."

"Right? So this is purely a hypothetical situation?"

"Yeah. Anyway, if word was to get out about the sup. Say you were to receive an anonymous tip-off — "

"Who from?"

"It's anonymous. Remember?"

"Sorry. My brain isn't in gear yet. Go on."

"If you got an anonymous tip-off, would you always act on it, or would it depend on the couple, and the particular circumstances?"

"I'd have no choice. I would have to act on it."

"That's pretty harsh."

"Those are the rules."

"Okay, well thanks for the info, Daze, and sorry for calling so early."

"That's okay. Just don't forget my invitation when you two tie the knot."

***

Mrs V and Jules were both at their desks. The first thing I noticed was that the filing cabinet had been moved back to its spot near the window. The next thing I noticed was the stupid grin on both of their faces.

"Something tells me you two have some good news."

"We won!" Jules blurted out.

"First prize in our classes." Mrs V was a little more reserved, but only slightly. "First in tea cosies for me."

"And first in hats for me."

"That's great. The identical patterns didn't come back to haunt you, then?"

"It may have worked against us in the overall competition." Mrs V conceded. "I came joint tenth."

"I came joint tenth too!" Jules said.

"Well done, both of you. You should be very proud."

I started for my office.

"Jill, hold on," Mrs V called after me. "You haven't forgotten our money, have you?"

"What money?"

"The money you were holding for our wager."

"I assumed that as there was no clear winner in the overall competition, I'd get to keep that."

They both gave me a look.

"Kidding. I was only kidding."

Drat! I almost got away with it.

Winky was under the sofa, snoring. I didn't want to disturb him, so I began to tiptoe over to my desk.

That's when I spotted it.

Bob, the dead spider, was on the floor, under the window sill. Poor Winky—Bob's death had hit him hard. Even so, I couldn't allow the body to litter the floor. I would be doing Winky a favour if I disposed of it. That way, he might begin to get over his loss. I took a tissue from my pocket and used it to pick up the poor little fellow.

Wait a minute! Something wasn't right. I opened up the tissue and stared at Bob.

Bob, the *plastic* spider!

"Winky! Get out here, right now!"

He crawled out from under the sofa, still bleary-eyed. "What do you want?"

"I just wanted to apologise once again for what happened with Bob. I still feel terrible about it."

"And so you should, but I'm sure with the right support, I'll get over it."

"By *support*, I assume you mean salmon?"

"Yes. That does seem to help."

"Okay. I'll get some for you now. While I do, would you mind holding this *plastic spider*?"

Winky stared in horror at the spider on the tissue. "Ahh,

right. I can explain."

"Talk to the hand because I'm finished listening to your lies. You have fooled me for the last time. I'm done with you. Do you hear?"

"Loud and clear. Sorry."

I went back to my desk.

"Does this mean that salmon is off the menu?" he said.

"Forever."

Never again would I fall for one of his stupid tricks.

Daze may have got the wrong end of the stick when I'd spoken to her, but she'd made it quite clear that if Blake's situation was made public, he'd be in for a whole world of hurt. I'd spent ages studying the blackmail note, but it had shed no clues on who the perpetrator might be. I decided to take a look through the blog which Jen had authored under the pseudonym of the Wizard's Wife. Even though she had subsequently removed the blog, it wasn't difficult to find a 'cached' version.

I spent the best part of two hours reading through every post. Apart from being mind-numbingly boring, I didn't find a single post which contained sufficient information to give away the author's identity. How then did the blackmailer identify Jen, and find out where she and Blake lived? It was always possible that Jen had said something out of turn IRL.

What? Of course I know what IRL means. I know *all* the acronyms. Oh, alright, if you must know, Jules told me that it stands for 'In Real Life'.

Anyway, if Jen had said something IRL, the chances of me ever tracking down the blackmailer were somewhere south of zero. I did have one hunch, but only one, and it was a long-shot. For Blake's sake, I hoped I was right.

***

Sounds coffee shop was located close to the Radio Wash studios. Lee Sparks' online diary had included an entry for a meeting there with his ex-manager, Raymond Conway, on the morning of the murder. So far, I'd drawn a blank trying to get hold of Conway, so I decided to pay a visit to the coffee shop instead. Maybe someone there would remember seeing the two men on that fateful day.

"Hi." The freckled-faced young man behind the counter had a gap between his two front teeth, which caused him to whistle when he spoke. "What can I get for you today?"

"A caramel latte, please."

"Anything to go with that?"

"Do you have any muffins?"

"Sorry. There's no call for them hereabouts."

No call for muffins? What kind of hell hole had I just crawled into. "What do you have?"

"Cookies, brownies, giant custard creams, cupcakes—"

"Whoa! Rewind! Did you say custard creams?"

"Yeah, but we don't have the regular ones. Just these giant ones." He pointed to a plateful of the largest custard creams I'd ever seen.

"I'll take one of those, please."

"There you go." He put it on a plate, and passed it to me. "I was beginning to think we'd made a mistake with these. That's the only one I've sold this week. Can I get you anything else?"

"Just some information. I'm investigating the Lee Sparks murder." I flashed him my business card. "Did he ever come in here?"

"He was always in here. Lee used to say that our coffee was the best he'd ever tasted. He often popped in on his way into the studio, and sometimes he would send his minions to get some for him."

"His *minions*?"

"I shouldn't call them that, but it's how Lee referred to them. He'd often send his producer or manager to pick up a coffee for him."

"Speaking of his manager, do you happen to recall seeing him and Lee in here on the day of the murder?"

"I'm not likely to forget it. They had a real slanging match. I had to have a word with them because they were upsetting the other customers."

"Any idea what they were arguing about?"

"Not really. By the time they started getting loud, they were just throwing insults at one another."

"Are you sure you can't remember anything specific that was said?"

"I don't want to get anyone into trouble."

"Provided you tell the truth, that won't happen."

"When his manager stormed out, he was still yelling at Lee. He said he was going to kill him, but people say that kind of thing all the time, don't they?"

***

I was on my way to Aunt Lucy's, and I was a little worried in case she and Monica had had a bust-up on their shopping expedition, and Aunt Lucy blamed me.

As soon as I walked through her front door, I could hear voices and laughter coming from the kitchen. That was a hopeful sign, at least. Even if the shopping trip had been a disaster, it sounded as though Aunt Lucy had got over it.

"Jill? Is it that time already? Come in."

As I stepped into the kitchen, I did a double-take. Seated at the table was Monica.

"Hi, Jill." She stood up. "I'd better get going. I only popped over for a quick chat with your Aunt."

"There's no need for you to rush off," Aunt Lucy said. "Stay a few more minutes."

"Thanks, but I have things I need to do. The cake was really lovely."

"Drop by anytime. Don't wait to be invited."

"Will do. Bye, then."

"I'm guessing the shopping expedition was a success?" I said, after Monica had left.

"It was a brilliant idea of yours, Jill. I've got the perfect dress, thanks to Monica."

"You two hit it off, then?"

"I don't mind admitting that I was wrong about that young lady. She's an absolute darling."

"Lester must have been pleased to hear you say that."

"He was, and I've apologised to him for being so unreasonable before. Anyway, would you like to see the dress?"

"I'd love to, but not right now. I'd like to get moving on the Best Cakes plan if you're still up for it."

"Definitely. I'm excited about helping, but I still don't know what you want me to do."

Chapter 15

"Are you sure this is going to work, Jill?" Aunt Lucy sounded much less enthusiastic after I'd outlined my brilliant (crazy?) plan.

"Absolutely." I figured if I sounded confident that she wouldn't realise I was just winging it.

"Okay, then. Shall I shrink myself now or do you want to wait until we get to Best Cakes?"

"It would probably be best to do it now, in case someone sees you."

"It's been a long time since I cast the 'shrink' spell." She sounded nervous. "I hope I can still remember how."

Moments later, she'd proven that her memory hadn't failed her.

"Brace yourself." I crouched down. "I'm going to pick you up now."

"Be gentle," she said, in a squeaky, little voice.

I grabbed hold of mini-Aunt Lucy, and put her in my pocket.

When I walked through the door of Best Cakes, the ice maidens glared at me.

"The bad penny is back," Laura said.

"Have you deserted Scuzzy C?" Flora laughed at her own joke.

"I'd like to take a look in your stock room."

"Why?"

"That's none of your business. Miles told you that I should have free access to all areas of the shop, didn't he?"

"Knock yourself out." Laura shrugged.

I made my way through to the stock room. Once in there, I had to act quickly because I knew the ice maidens might follow at any moment. After taking mini-Aunt Lucy out of my pocket, she reversed the 'shrink' spell to bring herself back to full-size.

Aunt Lucy went straight into action, hollowing out one of the large muffins, just as I'd instructed. When she'd finished, I sat on the counter, and shrank myself small enough to get inside the hollowed-out cake. There was just enough room inside for me to stand up. Aunt Lucy had remembered to make a small slot through which I could see.

"Ready, Jill?" she whispered to the muffin.

"Yes!" I had to shout to be heard.

I watched through the slot as Aunt Lucy cast the 'doppelganger' spell, to make herself look like me. Then, she hurried out of the stock room, and out of the shop. I'd given her strict instructions not to engage with the ice maidens on the way out. If my plan had worked, they would now believe that I'd left the premises. All I had to do now was wait.

Have you ever been stuck inside a muffin? Sorry— stupid question—of course you haven't. If you ever do find yourself in that predicament, you'll discover that there's a great temptation to take bites out of the muffin walls that surround you. Of course, being the professional I am, I managed to resist that temptation.

What? Who are you calling a liar? Okay, then, but it was only one or two bites. Maybe three.

An hour later, and I was still waiting. What if I'd got this badly wrong? It was getting awfully hot inside the cake, and I was really thirsty.

Just then, the door to the stock room opened, and in walked Flora. Suddenly, everything tilted to one side, and I realised that she'd picked up my muffin. I had to hold onto the sides, so that I didn't fall out. Fortunately, the cake was soon back on the level again. I was on a tray alongside lots of other cakes. If my hunch was right, any moment now she would start to insert pins into the cakes, and I would have her bang to rights.

Whoa! I had to grab the sides again when Flora picked up the tray, and carried it through to the shop. I'd been watching her, and so far, she hadn't pushed a pin into any of the cakes. That threw me a little because I'd been sure that the sabotage would take place in the stock room — out of sight of the customers. Once in the shop, she proceeded to place each cake into the display cabinet.

I now had to face the possibility that I'd got this completely wrong. Maybe the ice maidens weren't behind the sabotage after all? Either way, I now had a much bigger problem to worry about. Now that I was in the display cabinet, a customer could decide to buy my muffin at any moment. What would I do then? I'd have no choice but to blow my cover, and make my escape. The alternative was to become someone's snack.

Fortunately, Flora had placed my muffin at such an angle that I had a good view of the shop.

"Yes, madam?" Laura said when an elderly witch came to the counter.

"A cup of tea — milk no sugar, please."

"Anything with that?"

"I quite fancy a muffin."

Oh bum!

"Which flavour?"

Not the strawberry! Please, don't pick the strawberry!

"I'm torn between the chocolate and the strawberry."

Choose the chocolate one, please! The chocolate one looks lovely!

"I think I'll have the strawberry. No, wait! I'll have the chocolate."

Phew! That was too close for comfort.

Twenty minutes later, and I was still hanging in there. The shop looked to be deserted of customers, so maybe I'd get an opportunity to escape. If only there was some way I could distract the ice maidens.

"You two take a break while it's quiet," a familiar voice said.

It was Mindy. Thank goodness. Now I'd be able to escape from the muffin, and explain to her that I'd been carrying out surveillance.

Ouch! What the — ?

Something sharp had just stabbed my thigh. I moved over to the opposite side of the cake, and from there, I could see what had caused the stabbing pain. The tip of a pin was clearly visible, protruding through the wall of the muffin.

Mindy was the saboteur!

Another pin appeared through the cake wall; this one just missed my shoulder.

"Hey!" I screamed at the top of my voice. "Stop doing that!"

Everything went a bit crazy after that. Mindy must have been so surprised to hear the muffin talking to her that she dropped it. I was thrown back and forth as it hurtled to the ground. Fortunately, I wasn't thrown out.

By the time the cake hit the floor, I was somewhat

disorientated. I blame the dizziness on the decision I made next. I should have crawled out of the cake, and then reversed the 'shrink' spell. Instead, I reversed the 'shrink' spell first. As a consequence, the muffin exploded as I reverted to full size.

"Jill?" Mindy was so shocked that she dropped the remaining pin onto the floor.

"What are you playing at?" I said, while pulling pieces of strawberry muffin out of my hair.

"You were inside the muffin?"

"I was watching Flora and Laura, to try to catch them sabotaging your cakes, but now I find it was you all along."

She broke down in tears.

"Let's take a walk." I took her hand.

"What about the shop?"

"The ice maidens will be back out soon. Come on, let's find somewhere quiet where we can talk."

There was a small public garden just up the road from Best Cakes. On a quiet bench, I waited until Mindy had managed to compose herself.

"What's this all about, Mindy?"

"It's those two girls! You were right about them. They're evil!"

"What have they done?"

"They've both been coming on to Miles."

"Didn't he tell them to sling their hook?"

"He can't say no to a pretty face. He doesn't think I know, but I'm not stupid." She wiped away the tears, and took a deep breath. "I thought if I could frame them for the sabotage, he'd show them the door."

"I don't understand why you still want to be with him.

If he's prepared to cheat on you like that, he doesn't deserve you."

"Who else would want me?"

"Now you're being ridiculous. You're an intelligent, attractive woman; you could do a lot better than that slime ball. The sooner you dump him, the better."

"You're right. I know you are. I've been such a fool." She stood up. "But that's going to change."

"What are you going to do?"

"What I should have done a long time ago."

***

The blackmailer had threatened to give Blake and Jen up to the rogue retrievers unless Blake paid up. That wasn't an option because he didn't have the money, and even if he'd had it, the chances were that the blackmailer would keep coming back for more.

My one and only hunch was that the blackmailer must have got Jen's details from the blog. I'd read through all the posts she'd ever made as the Wizard's Wife, and they had given nothing away. That ruled out the many readers of the blog as suspects, but it didn't rule out whoever owned the website which hosted Washbridge Bloggers. To test my theory, I'd signed up for a blog on the same website. As part of the sign-up process, the user was required to enter their name and email address. Optionally, the user could also provide a physical address. Most people would have declined to give out that kind of information, but Jen had already proven herself to be somewhat naïve. What if she'd included all of her details when signing up? If she had, the owner of the website would have all the information he needed to blackmail her husband.

Tracing the owner of the website had been easy because the information was publicly available. He lived at Washbridge View—a small development of mews type houses, located close to the swimming baths.

I pressed the doorbell.

"Yes?" The young wizard who answered the door had huge nostrils. If he'd taken in a deep breath, I would probably have been sucked up into his sinuses.

"Colin Spikes?"

"Who wants to know?"

I glanced around. "I'm pretty sure that would be me."

"I don't have time for smartasses. What do you want?"

"I believe you run the Washbridge Bloggers website?"

"Nah. Nothing to do with me." He started to close the door, but I stuck my foot in the gap.

"Not so quick, Colin. Let me rephrase that. I *know* you run the website. I have the printout of the domain record in my pocket, if you'd like to see it."

"So what if I do? The web site is perfectly legal."

"It's not the website I'm here to discuss."

"What do you want, then? Who are you, anyway?"

"I'm the person who is going to inform the rogue retrievers that you are a blackmailer."

"That's rubbish!"

"Do you know Daze?"

"Everyone knows Daze."

"She just happens to be a close personal friend of mine. One phone call, and she'll be here in a matter of minutes. You can tell her that you're not involved with blackmail, and then I'll show her my evidence. We'll see who she believes, shall we?"

"No! There's no need for that. It wasn't really blackmail. It was just a joke. A bit of a laugh."

"Do I look like I'm laughing?"

"I'm sorry. Please don't call Daze."

"The person you were trying to blackmail is one of my neighbours. When I leave here, I'm going to tell him that he won't hear any more from the blackmailer, but that if he does, he should tell me straightaway. And guess what I'll do then?"

"He won't hear from me again. I promise."

"Good boy."

Those nostrils would give me nightmares for years to come.

Chapter 16

Arranging a meeting with Mike Spins had proven to be remarkably easy. I'd heard that the man was something of a narcissist, and so it had turned out. We met in the small staff canteen at the radio station, and once I'd told him that I was a huge fan, I had him eating out of my hand.

"You're rather younger than most of my fans," he said.

"I started listening when I was a kid. I was very disappointed when they took you off the drivetime show."

"You and thousands of others, but don't worry. It's only a matter of time until they restore me to my rightful slot." Then as an afterthought. "Of course, I wouldn't have wanted it to happen under such tragic circumstances."

"Of course not. I wasn't a fan of Lee Sparks, but nobody deserves to die like that."

"Quite." He took out a nail file, and began to file his fingernails. He was clearly devastated by his young colleague's untimely death.

"I understand that you and Lee Sparks had a meeting on the morning of the day he was murdered."

"We did indeed. We sat at this very table, as it happens."

"What was your meeting about, if you don't mind me asking?"

"Not at all. I have nothing to hide. Lee wanted to pick my brain."

"Oh? What about?"

"Lee might have been popular, but I have something he didn't." He paused for effect. "Experience. Lee was worried that the ratings on the drivetime show might fall, so he was asking my advice on how to retain the audience."

"And were you able to help him?"

"Of course. I'm a generous man. Everyone will tell you that. I was able to give Lee a few tips." He sighed. "Not that it will do him any good now."

On my previous visit, Susie Bubbly had told me that there was only the one entrance to the radio station. But should I really trust the word of a woman with the memory of a goldfish? Probably not.

After leaving through the main doors, I took a walk around the perimeter. It was just as well that I had because at the rear of the building I found a metal door with a combination lock. I was just about to return to reception, to ask Susie about the door, when it opened.

Both I and the young woman jumped.

"What are you doing back here?" She eyed me suspiciously.

"Sorry if I scared you. My name is Jill Gooder. I'm a private investigator. I'm looking into the murder of Lee Sparks. Can I ask your name?"

"Jenny Black. It's a terrible business. Everyone's been on edge since it happened."

"What do you do here, Jenny?"

"I'm a cleaner."

"Did you know Lee?"

"I wouldn't say I 'knew' him, exactly, but I did see him most days."

"What did you make of him?"

"Not much. A bit of a prat if you ask me. He used to call us by our surnames as though we were his servants."

"Us?"

"Me and the other cleaners."

"How many of you are there?"

"Three altogether. Me, Carol and Mrs Draycott—she's the boss. Sparks was always barking something at us: *this table is dusty, Black. My bin hasn't been emptied, Draycott.* If I didn't need this job so bad, I'd have flattened him."

"Do you always use this door?"

"We have no choice. The management don't want the likes of us to be seen out front."

"Does anyone else use it?"

"I don't think so, but you'd be better off asking Mrs Draycott; she'd know for sure."

"Is she in today?"

"She's off ill. The runs, I think."

"Do you happen to have a number where I can contact her?"

"Sure."

I thanked Jenny for her help, and then continued my inspection of the building. There were no more doors, and no other obvious ways to gain entry.

I was on my way back to the car when I heard footsteps. I turned around to find a woman hurrying after me.

"Can I have a word?" she said, while trying to catch her breath.

"You are?"

"Patty Phillips. I work as a secretary here. Could we talk somewhere else?"

"Sure. How about the coffee shop just down the road?"

"Okay."

At Sounds coffee shop, I ordered the drinks, and then

we found a quiet table. It wasn't difficult because the place was deserted.

I overheard what Mike said to you in the canteen earlier. It was a pack of lies."

"Oh?"

"Lee was a wonderful performer. Unique. He had more talent in his little finger than that old has-been ever had. The idea that Lee would have gone to him for advice is ridiculous. Mike hasn't had an original idea for years."

"Did you hear what they were talking about?"

"There wasn't much talking going on. They were shouting at one another. Mike wanted Lee to host a joint program with him, but Lee laughed in his face. Why would he work with that old timer?"

"Did they come to blows?"

"No, but Mike said that Lee would get his comeuppance, and that he'd see he did."

"Did he say it in such a way that it sounded like a serious threat?"

"I would say so."

"Did you know Lee Sparks well?"

"We were friends. I never understood why so many people had it in for him. Jealousy, if you ask me."

Patty went on to detail all the qualities she'd admired in Lee Sparks, and it soon became apparent that she'd had a serious crush on him.

So far, I'd heard from the coffee shop owner who'd said that Lee Sparks had argued with his ex-manager on the morning of the murder. Understandably, Raymond Conway hadn't been thrilled at being sacked by Sparks. Patty Phillips had suggested the meeting between Sparks and Mike Spins had been far from a friendly affair. Mike Spins can't have been happy when Sparks threw the idea of a joint show back in his face. The number of people with a motive to murder Sparks was slowly mounting.

***

I went back to the office because I wasn't in any particular hurry to get home where Jack's mother would be waiting. For some reason, she'd taken against me. I'd watched her during the anniversary party, and she'd made a point of talking to everyone. Everyone except me. Sure, she'd greeted me when we arrived, but after that it was as though she was doing her best to avoid me.

Why had she suddenly decided to pay us a visit? She'd had over a year to come to our house, but hadn't shown any interest in doing so. I was convinced that she'd decided I wasn't good enough for her son (which was probably true), and had decided to do something about it before it was too late. If that was the case, she'd underestimated me. I didn't intend to give up Jack without a fight.

Winky couldn't have looked any guiltier if he'd tried.

"What are you up to?"

"Nothing." He had his paws behind his back again, as though he was trying to hide something.

"Okay."

I was onto his game. He obviously wanted me to ask what he was hiding, but I wasn't going to fall for his tricks ever again. Whatever he was up to was of zero interest to me.

"Honestly," he said. "I'm not up to anything."

"I believe you."

"And there's nothing behind my back."

"Good. Now, if you don't mind, I have cases to review."

It had taken me a long time, but I'd finally got the measure of that cat.

My phone rang; it was Grandma.

"Tell her I agree," she said.

"Sorry? Tell who you agree to what?"

"That sister of yours. Tell her I agree to the pay rise for her and whatshername."

"Chloe."

"Whatever. Tell her that I expect them both to be here tomorrow."

"Why the change of mind? Didn't the temporary staff work out?"

"The temps were perfectly fine. I've just carried out a strategic review of the shop's operations, and decided that it's in the long-term interest of the business to increase payroll for key operatives."

That woman was so full of it.

"I can tell Kathy that she's now considered a key operative, can I?"

"You can tell her what you like, just so long as you make sure she's in this shop tomorrow morning."

"It will be my pleasure, Grandma."

She'd already ended the call, so I immediately phoned Kathy.

"You won!"

"What?"

"Grandma just caved in. She's going to give you and

Chloe the pay rise you asked for."

"How do you know?"

"She just rang me."

"How come she didn't call *me*?"

"Because she didn't want to lose face, probably. And get this—she called you a 'key operative'."

"That's fantastic news. I was really worried how we were going to make ends meet without my wages."

"Did you see the temps she got in?"

"No. I haven't been near the shop since she sacked us."

"Between you and me, you have them to thank for this. *Useless* doesn't come close. Anyway, you have to report for work as normal tomorrow morning."

"That's great. I'll call Chloe now with the good news."

***

I could put it off no longer. It was time to go home to face Jack's mother, and my destiny. Would Jack and I still be an item in the morning? If I had anything to do with it, then the answer was most definitely 'yes'.

Bring it on, Mrs Maxwell.

I pulled onto the driveway, took a deep breath, and climbed out of the car. I was prepared for whatever she had to throw at me.

"Jill!" Blake came hurrying across the road towards me. "Sorry to trouble you, but I'm getting really worried."

"You can relax. You won't be hearing any more from the blackmailer."

"How can you be so sure?"

"Because I threatened him with the rogue retrievers."

"Who was it?"

"A wizard with big nostrils. He's the guy who runs the bloggers website. Jen must have entered her full details, including her address, when she signed up."

"What was she thinking?" Blake shook his head.

"Don't be too hard on her. Remember you'd just dropped the '*I'm a wizard*' bombshell. She probably wasn't thinking straight."

"You're right. It's as much my fault as hers. Are you sure we're safe now?"

"Positive. Just keep an eye on Jen, and make sure she doesn't do anything stupid."

"Don't worry. I will."

Jack was waiting for me just inside the door. "Mum is in the lounge."

"Right."

His mother was sitting on the sofa.

"Hello, Mrs Maxwell."

"Please call me Yvonne. Mrs Maxwell makes me sound ancient."

"Okay, Yvonne."

"I'll make dinner," Jack said. "That'll give you two time to talk."

"Jack," Yvonne said. "What are you planning for dinner?"

"I bought steak."

"Oh."

"Why? Was there something else you'd prefer?"

"I quite fancy tuna bake."

"I don't think we have any tuna."

"I'll go and get some." I volunteered. Any excuse to

escape for a few minutes.

"No, Jill," Yvonne said. "You stay and talk to me. Jack will go to the shop, won't you, dear?"

"Err—yes, of course. I won't be long."

I knew it. She'd taken the first opportunity to get Jack out of the house. This is where she got to tell me what she really thought of me. To tell me why I wasn't worthy of her son.

"I wanted to speak to you alone," she said, as soon as Jack had left.

"Why don't you start by telling me why you don't like me? What did I do wrong?"

"What?" She looked stunned. She'd obviously expected me to roll over, but she was in for a fight. "Of course I like you. You're possibly the best thing that's ever happened to Jack. It's obvious to anyone how much he loves you."

What kind of tactic was this? Was she trying to lull me into a false sense of security, so that she could strike a fatal blow?

"You practically ignored me the whole time I was at your house for the party. You barely spoke to me."

"I know, and I'm so sorry. It's just that when you and your family arrived, I simply wasn't prepared."

"Wasn't prepared for what?"

She glanced at the door. Whatever she was about to say, she obviously didn't want Jack to hear.

"I had no idea that you and your relatives were witches."

I felt as though the air had been punched out of me. "Sorry? What did you just say?"

"I know you're a sup, Jill. And so are your grandmother, aunt and cousins."

This didn't make any sense. Yvonne wasn't a sup, or I'd have sensed it. How could she possibly know?

"I have no idea what you're talking about." I had to brazen it out.

"There's something I need to show you, but before I do, you have to trust me when I say that you have absolutely nothing to fear from me. Do you trust me, Jill?"

"Err—yes, I suppose so."

"I have to be sure."

"Okay. I trust you. Now, what is it?"

She leaned forward, and appeared to peel back a small section of skin from the nape of her neck. That's when I saw the small tattoo of a goblet.

She was a witchfinder!

Chapter 17

The next morning, as soon as I woke, the events of the previous evening came flooding back to me. What a revelation! Yvonne and I hadn't had long to talk before Jack came back from the shop, but it had been long enough for her to drop a bombshell into my life.

I'd assumed she'd ignored me at the anniversary party because she didn't like me, and thought I was an unsuitable partner for her son. In fact, our arrival at her house had rocked her world. Until then, she'd had no idea that I and my birth family were sups. Given the circumstances, she'd coped with the evening remarkably well.

When she'd first disclosed that she was a witchfinder, I'd been shocked, and feared for my safety, but Yvonne had put my mind at ease by explaining that she had in fact retired many years earlier. I still had lots of questions, and I didn't intend to go to work until I'd had the chance to have a proper heart-to-heart with her.

I showered, dressed and went downstairs to find Jack and his mother sitting at the breakfast bar. They were both eating muesli.

"Care for some?" Jack offered the box.

"No, thanks. Morning, Yvonne."

"Morning, Jill."

"Mum and I have just been talking about you." Jack grinned.

"Should I be worried?"

"Not at all." Yvonne gave me a reassuring smile, and if I wasn't mistaken, a wink. "I was just saying how much I admire the work that you do, Jill. It can't be an easy job."

"The hardest part is having to deal with certain members of the police force." I looked at Jack. "Some of them can be a real pain in the bum."

Yvonne laughed. "From what I hear, you can give as good as you get."

"Better, if you ask me," Jack said. "Anyway, I'd better be making tracks." He gave his mum a peck on the cheek. "See you tonight, Mum."

"Bye, darling."

"And you." He gave me a quick kiss on the lips. "Take care."

"You too."

Yvonne and I exchanged a glance, and waited until we heard the door close.

"I imagine you have a lot of questions?" she said.

That was the understatement of the year—where to begin?

"I assume that Jack doesn't know—that you're a—err—?"

"Witchfinder? It's okay to say it. No, he knows nothing about it. Neither does his father, come to that."

"That's incredible. How have you managed to live together for so long and keep that secret?"

"I'm surprised you have to ask. Aren't you in exactly the same position?"

"I suppose so. I hadn't thought of it like that."

"If anything, it must be even more difficult for you, Jill. You have the rogue retrievers to worry about."

"You know about them?"

"Of course. There isn't much about the sup world I don't know."

"How did you become a witchfinder?"

"Both of my parents were in the business, and I just followed suit, but I hated the job, and the life. Don't get me wrong, I was good at it, but after a few years, I realised it wasn't for me. When I met Jack's father, we fell madly in love. After we were married, I continued in the business, but as soon as Jack was born, I gave it all up. I was adamant that no child of mine would have to do what I had done."

"Were there any consequences to your decision to retire?"

"No, and there won't be just so long as I never reveal what I am to anyone."

"But you've told me."

"You're the only person I have ever told."

"Will you get into trouble?"

"Not unless you decide to make the information public."

"I would never do that. What made you decide to tell me?"

"I could see what you and Jack have is special, and I want to be a part of that. It's one thing keeping my secret from humans, but how could I keep it from a witch? If I had, and you'd found out, it would have destroyed your trust in me forever. I was very nervous about telling you, though."

"Why?"

"Isn't it obvious? I wouldn't blame you for hating witchfinders. After all, their job is to destroy you."

"You're only the second one I've ever met. My encounter with the first one didn't end well—for him. But you're retired."

"Are you comfortable knowing what I used to do?"

"I don't see why not, although it probably wouldn't be a good idea for me to tell the rest of my family, and especially not Grandma."

"I thought she and I really hit it off at the party. Although, for some reason, she seemed to think that I was teetotal."

"That is weird. I still think it would be better to keep this between the two of us."

"I'm happy to go along with whatever you think is best."

"Doesn't it bother you that your son is sharing his life with a sup?"

"Why would it?" She shrugged. "My only concern is his happiness, and you obviously make him happy. It doesn't matter whether you're a human or a sup."

"That's good to hear."

"Do you think you will ever tell him?"

"I don't think so. I don't see what good could come of it. Don't get me wrong, I hate having secrets from Jack, but on balance, I think it's for the best."

"I'm so glad we've cleared the air." She leaned over and put her arms around me.

"Me too. Do you mind if I ask you a couple more questions?"

"Of course not. Go ahead."

"Why haven't you had the tattoo removed? Aren't you afraid someone might see it?"

"The goblet isn't a normal tattoo; there's no way to remove it. The 'plaster' that covers it is made of synthetic skin. It's undetectable even to the medical profession. It's held in place by a potion known only to witchfinders, so there's no danger it will ever come off. I'm the only person who can remove it."

"Are there many retired witchfinders?"

"Very few. Most remain in the job until they die."

"I see."

"You haven't asked the one question that I expected you to ask."

"What's that?"

"How many witches did I destroy?"

"I don't need to know. Your past life is just that—in the past."

***

I would have liked to talk to Yvonne for much longer, but I'd arranged a meeting with Raymond Conway, Lee Sparks' ex-manager. My head was still spinning from the revelation that Jack's mother was a retired witchfinder. I probably should have been horrified, but I was actually quite relieved. I'd been worried that she didn't like me, and didn't think I was good enough for Jack. The fact that Yvonne was willing to reveal her secret to me proved beyond any doubt that wasn't the case.

I had to smile when I thought about Jack's part in all of this. He was living with a witch, and had a retired witchfinder for a mother. And he was blissfully unaware of it all.

What a weird world we lived in.

Raymond Conway's office made mine look palatial. It was a grubby room in a grubby building. And in keeping with his surroundings, Raymond Conway's appearance gave grubby a bad name.

"What's this about? I'm a busy man."

If the room had been bigger, I might have stood a better chance of getting out of halitosis range. As it was, I just had to hold my breath for as long as I could.

"I understand that you had a meeting in Sounds coffee shop with Lee Sparks on the morning of the day that he was murdered."

"Might have." He shrugged. "I have a lot of meetings with a lot of people."

"I've spoken to a witness who said the two of you were arguing."

"We were always arguing."

"I believe Lee had recently dispensed with your services?"

"Don't believe everything you hear. I was the one who fired him. The little toe-rag was more trouble than he was worth. Thought he was something special, that one. When you've been in this game as long as I have, you see them come, and you see them go, but Ray Conway is still standing."

"Still, you can't have been pleased to have lost your cut of his earnings?"

"Lee Sparks was an arrogant punk. I was glad to see the back of him."

"The witness said they heard you threaten to kill him."

"I don't believe I said that, but even if I did, it meant nothing. I wouldn't have sullied my hands on that waste of space."

"Where were you the rest of that day?"

"Henry's, most likely."

"Henry's?"

"It's the bar three doors down."

"And you were there all day?"

"Probably."

It was great to get back out into the fresh air. I wasn't sure what to make of Conway. His alibi was hardly watertight, and he definitely hadn't been a fan of Lee Sparks. But a murderer? I wasn't convinced.

***

I'd been so busy talking to Yvonne earlier that I hadn't got around to grabbing any breakfast. I was starving, and I knew what would fill the gap nicely. I'll give you a clue: it starts with an 'M' and ends with an 'N'.

The twins were behind the tea room counter in Cuppy C, and both of them looked like they'd just lost the winning lottery ticket.

"What's wrong, girls?"

"It's the drive-thru hatch," Pearl said.

"What's wrong with it?"

"How were we supposed to know that the ground level in the alleyway is higher than the level of the floor here in Cuppy C?"

"Sorry, girls, I'm really not following any of this."

"Come and see." They led the way to the back of the shop.

"That hatch looks rather high up."

"Duh? What do you think we've just been saying?" Amber went over and stood next to it. The bottom of the opening was almost level with the top of her head.

"How are you going to serve the customers?" I laughed.

"I'm glad you think it's funny, Jill." Pearl glared at me.

"Sorry. It obviously isn't funny." More laughter. "At all."

They were both glaring at me.

"Can't you get the builders to come back and lower it?"

"Then it will be too low on the other side."

"What are you going to do, then?"

Amber walked over to the cupboard, and came back with a small stepladder.

At that, I dissolved into laughter.

The twins were obviously not amused, and stormed back into the shop. It was several minutes before I felt confident enough to follow them inside. If I laughed again, I would be dead meat.

"Sorry about that," I said, with a straight face. "This must be very annoying."

"It is," Amber said. "But the stepladder should work until we can get a raised platform put in at this side."

"Good idea. I'm really sorry that I laughed. Now, can I get a caramel latte and a blueberry muffin, please?"

Daze was by herself at the window table.

"Do you mind if I join you?"

"Of course not. What was going on out back? I could hear you laughing from here."

Moments later, the two of us were crying with laughter.

"A stepladder?" Daze managed through the tears.

"Shush! Don't let the twins hear you, or they'll never serve me again."

"You couldn't make this stuff up. Do you remember the conveyor belt they had installed?"

"How could I forget? And what about that chocolate fountain?"

Chapter 18

While I was in Candlefield, I decided to pay a visit to the Museum of Witchcraft, which was situated on the spot where Magna Mondale's house had once stood. The original basement was still beneath the museum, and it was there that the 'sealed' room was located. Many witches had tried to enter it, but I'd been the one who had finally managed to get inside. That's where I'd found Magna Mondale's spell book, which had played a major part in advancing my magic skills. I thought I'd seen the last of that room, but according to Imelda Barrowtop's journal, Magna had left a message in there. A message intended for whoever had eventually broken the seal to the room. A message intended for me.

I wasn't sure if the young woman on reception was actually awake.

"Hello?"

"Sorry." She jumped. "I was day dreaming. Just a minute. I know you. You're Jill Gooder."

"That's right."

"What an honour." She stood up, and shook my hand. "I'm a big fan."

"Thank you." I found this kind of attention incredibly embarrassing. "I wondered if I could take a look in the basement? In the sealed room?"

"You know it's been sealed again, don't you?"

"Yes, I did hear about that, but this is rather important."

"No one is allowed in there, but I'm sure they'll make an exception for you. Can you just hold on a moment while I check with someone?"

"Of course."

She picked up the phone and punched three numbers.

"Ms Fish? It's Lottie. Yes, I know you said you weren't to be disturbed, but I have someone here who wants to go into the sealed room. Yes, I know that no one is allowed in there, but it's Jill Gooder. Yes, I'm sure it's her. Right. Okay, thanks." Lottie replaced the receiver, and turned to me. "Ms Fish is coming down to see you."

"Thanks." I'd met Coral Fish on my previous visits to the museum.

"While you wait, would you mind signing this?" Lottie took out a small notepad from her bag.

"Of course." I scribbled my name onto the blank page.

"My mum won't believe it when I tell her that I've met you."

"Jill, how lovely to see you, again." Coral Fish appeared through a door to my right. "Lottie tells me you want to enter the sealed room. May I ask why?"

"I'm sorry but I'm not at liberty to say."

"Not to worry. You're more than welcome to look inside. It has been sealed again, but I don't imagine that will prove a problem for you." She smiled. "I would just ask that you seal it again afterwards."

"Of course."

Coral led the way down to the basement. "We had this put up in your honour." She pointed to a small plaque on the wall next to the door. It read: *This room was sealed by Magna Mondale, and remained sealed until it was opened by Jill Gooder—the most powerful witch that Candlefield has ever known.*

"That's very flattering, but I'm not sure it's true."

"Would you like me to stay with you, or would you prefer to be left alone?"

"I'd like to do this by myself, if I may?"

"Of course."

Unsealing the door was a trivial matter. Inside, the room was just as spartan as I remembered it. Where was the message? I hadn't noticed anything the last time I'd been in there, but then I hadn't been looking for it. I'd been much more interested in Magna's book of spells.

The room was dark except for the light that shone through the open door, so I took out my phone, and activated the torch app. The only furniture in the room was the table on which Magna's book had rested for so many years. That was the obvious starting point, so I studied every square inch of it. I checked the underside and the legs, but there was no sign of a message of any kind. That left only the floor, walls and ceiling. I started in one corner of the room, and shone the torch at the ceiling, and then the wall from top to bottom. There were a few scratches and chips, but nothing that resembled a message. It was a tedious process, but I made my way slowly around the walls. Next, I checked every square inch of the floor. When I'd finished, my back was killing me, and still I'd found nothing. It seemed I wasn't destined to read Magna's message.

By the time I headed for the door, I was tired and covered in dust. What a complete waste of time that had been.

And then I saw it.

On the back of the door, right at the very top, someone had carved words into the wood. The message was very small, but I managed to read it: *Three chances, but no more. Find the first.*

Thanks for that, Magna. What was I supposed to make

of that cryptic nonsense? If I didn't know better, I'd have thought that someone was having a laugh at my expense.

***

I magicked myself back to Washbridge.

"What happened to you?" Grandma was seated in the outer office.

"What do you mean?" Then I realised I was still covered in dust. "I—err—had to go up into the attic for something."

"You might at least have changed your clothes before you came into work. What kind of impression do you think that will give your clients?"

"Was there something you wanted, Grandma?"

"It's a private matter."

Mrs V and Jules both had their heads down, as though they were busy with their work. I knew better.

"Come through to my office, then."

As soon as Winky saw Grandma, he dashed for cover under the sofa.

"Why do you have two receptionists?"

"Mrs V doesn't like to stay at home."

"It's time that old woman retired."

Pot? Kettle?

"I'm glad you came to your senses and gave Kathy and Chloe a pay rise."

"Maybe you should follow suit. You could start by paying Annabel a wage."

"We've had this conversation before. Mrs V works for free voluntarily."

"So says you."

"You wanted to talk to me about something?"

"I need you to take my photograph."

"Why come all the way up here to ask *me*? You could have got Kathy to take it. What do you want a photograph for, anyway?"

"It's a matter of the highest confidentiality, which is why I'd prefer you to take it."

"Because of my reputation for honesty and discretion?"

"No. It's because I have more to blackmail you with."

"What do you need a photo for? You must have dozens."

"I need a current one, and before I tell you why, I need to swear you to secrecy. You can't tell anyone."

"I promise I won't say a word."

"Do you swear on your future blueberry muffins?"

"Yes, okay. What's this all about?"

She handed me a newspaper cutting.

"You're going to audition for this?"

"Why not? I'd be ideal."

"You do realise that this is a professional production being made by a big studio? And, it's an open audition, so there'll be a lot of competition."

"That may be so, but if you take the trouble to read it thoroughly, you'll see they want to cast a newcomer in the part. They're looking for someone to play the matriarchal head of a family of witches. That's me to a T."

"Have you ever done any acting?"

"I'll have you know I used to be the star of CWADS."

"What's CWADS?"

"Candlefield Witches Amateur Dramatic Society."

"I've never heard you mention that before. When was it?"

"A few centuries ago, but what does that have to do with the price of fish? Are you going to take this photo or not?"

"Okay. Stand still, then."

"Make sure you get my best side."

Did she have one?

What? Harsh, but true.

"I assume it's a horror movie?" Winky slid out from under the sofa, as soon as Grandma had left.

"That's rather unkind."

"It's no worse than you were thinking. Can you imagine her face on the big screen? It would be enough to put you off your popcorn."

"Now you're just being cruel."

***

Hilary (Hills) Portman had been served a restraining order to stop her going anywhere near Lee Sparks. That meant she was definitely someone I needed to speak to.

The woman who answered the door was fifty if she was a day—much older than I'd expected.

"Hilary?"

"Nah. I'm Martha. Hills is my daughter. Are you that private whatsit that rang?"

"Yes. Jill Gooder."

"You'd better come in." She looked upstairs, and shouted, "Hills! That private thingy is here."

"Tell her to come up!" A deep voice came from somewhere above.

"It's the second door on the left. I was just about to have

a pickled egg. Do you want one?"

"Not for me, thanks. Second on the left, you said?"

"Yeah. Don't go in the first door whatever you do."

I didn't like to ask why.

The multi-coloured sign on the door read: Sparksville. I knocked.

"Come in."

"Hilary?"

"Hills. Everyone calls me Hills."

"Okay." I scanned the room; it was a shrine to Lee Sparks. Every inch of wall was covered with pictures of him. Some of them had been cut from newspapers or magazines — others had obviously been taken by Hills. There were at least a dozen selfies of her standing next to Lee Sparks. In a few of them, he was smiling, but in others he looked uncomfortable or annoyed. "You were a big fan, then?"

"His biggest fan. I worshipped him. I was a fan even before he moved to Radio Wash. I couldn't believe my luck when I found out they'd signed him. He loved me, you know."

"Did he tell you that?"

"He didn't need to. It was obvious."

"Didn't he have a girlfriend?"

"That was just for show. Lee didn't care about her."

"If Lee loved you, why did he take out a restraining order?"

"That was his so-called girlfriend's doing. She talked him into it. And do you know why she did it?"

"Why?"

"Because she knew how he felt about me."

"Right. How long has the restraining order been in

place?"

"A couple of months."

"So you won't have seen him for a while."

"Officially, no." She grinned.

"Unofficially?"

"I wasn't going to let a little thing like that come between me and Lee, so I used to go to the radio station in disguise."

"What kind of disguise?"

"I used lots of them. One time I borrowed my brother's overalls, and pretended to be checking the drains outside the radio station. Another time, I nicked all my mum's brollies—she's got tons of them. I set up a market stall outside the radio station."

"Wasn't anyone suspicious?"

"Nah, I even sold a couple of brollies."

"His death must have come as a devastating blow?"

"I can't believe he's gone. I still tune into the drivetime show every day. I keep thinking I'll hear his voice."

"Do you remember where you were on the day he died?"

"I was down the canal."

"Doing what?"

"I like to watch the ducks. They make me laugh. Have you seen the way they stick their bums up in the air?"

"Err—yeah."

"Hilarious, isn't it?"

"I suppose so. Do you often go down to the canal to watch the ducks?"

"Not often. Only three or four times a week."

"Right. And how long were you there that day?"

"I'm usually there all day, unless it rains. Or snows. Or

if it's foggy."

"Okay. Well, thank you for your help, Hills. Is it okay if I come back if I think of any more questions?"

"Sure. If I'm not here, you know where to find me."

"Down the canal?"

Hills Portman was obviously a few feathers short of a duck's bum, but she didn't strike me as a murderer.

"You done?" Hills' mother was at the bottom of the stairs.

"Yes, thanks."

"Are you sure you don't want a pickled egg?"

Chapter 19

The next morning, Jack was in the kitchen, making a fry-up for the three of us. Yvonne and I were in the lounge.

"I'm sorry you have to leave so soon, Yvonne." Those were words I had never expected to be saying.

"Me too, but Malcolm doesn't cope well on his own." She grinned. "Typical man."

"You must visit again, soon."

"I will. We both will next time. And you and Jack should come and stay with us."

"I'd like that."

Jack's mother had only been with us for a couple of days, but in that time, we'd formed a close bond. We did after all have something in common; we both had a secret that we could never reveal to Jack.

"Breakfast is served," Jack called from the kitchen.

"That looks good," Yvonne said, as we took our seats around the table. "I bet it makes a nice change to have Jack make the meals, doesn't it, Jill?"

"Definitely. I didn't think he knew where the pans were kept."

Jack shot me a look of disbelief.

"These sausages are delicious." Yvonne nodded her approval.

"I should eat them quickly before Jack snatches them off your plate, and throws them away."

"Ignore her, Mum. If it was up to Jill, we'd still be eating them after they'd turned green."

Thirty minutes later, it was time for Yvonne to leave.

Jack was going to run her to the station, on his way to work.

"Give me a hug." Yvonne threw her arms around me.

"See you soon."

She followed Jack out to the car, and I waved them off from the driveway. When I got back into the house, my phone rang. It was Kathy.

"Is she still there?"

"Jack's mother? No, he's just taken her to the station."

"So? Does she hate you?"

"No. She's an absolute darling."

"So, once again your paranoia was unfounded?"

"Seems that way."

"You had her down as a real witch."

"Finder."

"Sorry?"

"Never mind. I was one hundred per cent wrong about her. Yvonne is lovely. She can visit us any time she wants. Is that why you rang? To check if Jack and I were still together?"

"Of course not. I knew it was all in your imagination. I called because I wanted to ask if you knew that Washbridge House is supposed to be haunted?"

"I can't say I'd heard."

"Some of the people who work there mentioned it to Pete, and like a fool he told me in front of Lizzie. You know what she's like when it comes to ghosts. Now she's pestering me to take her there."

"Do they allow members of the public in?"

"According to Pete, they run tours of the house at certain times of the year."

"Why not take her then? It can't do any harm."

"Well, here's the thing. She said she'd like to go on the tour with you and Mad. She reckons that you two believe in ghosts, but I don't. What do you think? Would you and Mad be up for it?"

"I guess so, but I'll have to check to see when Mad is free. I'll let you know."

"That's great. And by way of a thank you, I thought I could treat you to lunch."

"*You* treat *me*?"

"You don't have to sound quite so shocked."

"But I am. When was the last time you bought lunch for me?"

"Do you fancy it or not?"

"Sure. I'd better say 'yes' before you change your mind. When?"

"How about today? We could go to that new place near Bar Piranha. I think it's called Chess."

"It's not some sleazy male strip club, is it?"

"*Chess*, Jill. Not *Chest*."

"Oh, sorry. Sure, why not?"

"Great. How about we meet outside there at midday?"

"Okay, I'll be there."

"Oh, Jill, there's just one more thing."

"Yeah?"

"Lolly Jolly will be joining us."

"What?" I screamed into the phone, but it was too late; she'd hung up.

Kathy. Was. So. Dead.

***

There were two women behind the desks in the outer

office, but neither of them was Mrs V.

"Jill, this is my sister," Jules said.

"Nice to meet you, err — ?"

"Lulu, but everyone calls me Lules."

Jules and Lules?

"Are you two twins?"

"No. Everyone thinks that, but I'm two years older," Jules said.

"You are very much alike."

"Lules still works at the black pudding factory where I used to work."

"Nice. Packing department?"

"No. I'm in quality control."

"That must be a very responsible job?"

"It's pretty boring, actually. I'm hoping to get into modelling."

"Lules just won Miss Black Pudding 2017." Jules was obviously proud of her younger sister.

"Congratulations. You're certainly pretty enough to be a model."

"Thanks." Lules blushed. "The problem is, I don't know how to get started."

"I might be able to help."

"Really? How?"

"My next-door neighbour is a model, although she is looking to get out of the business. I could ask her if she has any tips."

"Would you? That would be great."

"Sure. I'll pass on any info via Jules."

"Thanks, Jill. Jules told me what a great boss you are."

Winky was still acting very suspiciously. As soon as I

walked into the office, he hid a piece of paper in the lining on the underside of the sofa. He must have thought I'd just rolled in on the stupid train because it was painfully obvious that he'd wanted me to catch him doing it. He was going to be very disappointed because I wasn't falling for any of his tricks ever again.

I'd had an email from Luther, headed 'Year-end accounts'. The subject line alone was enough to send a shiver down my spine. I was tempted to press 'delete', and pretend I'd never seen it, but that was only putting off the inevitable.

I opened the email which read:

Jill
I have prepared provisional accounts for this financial year. I think we need to discuss these as a matter of urgency.
Luther

Maybe he wanted to congratulate me on the stellar year I'd had. Or maybe not.

I hit reply.

Luther
Thanks for the email. Very busy at the moment. Will contact you later to discuss accounts.
Jill

What? Who are you calling an ostrich?

***

I magicked myself over to GT where I'd arranged to meet Blodwyn at my father's house.

"Come in, Jill."

"Where's Dad?"

"He's still not very happy about me doing this. We had a big argument this morning, and he stormed out."

"I'm really sorry about that. I'll totally understand if you want to drop out."

"Definitely not. This is a good thing you're doing, and if I can help, I want to. Josh will just have to lump it. How exactly is this going to work?"

"I need you to take this." I took out the sachet of powder that I'd prepared earlier.

"What's that for?" She pulled a face.

"It will allow me to track your whereabouts when they transport you over to the human world."

"I thought I'd be wearing some kind of tracking device."

"I discussed this with one of my colleagues; she convinced me that the people behind this trade will have the means to check for any conventional tracking device. That's why I came up with this solution."

"What is it?"

"The powder is tasteless. I've cast a spell on it, so that I'll be able to track you down."

"I'm not very good at taking medicine."

"Just sprinkle it into a glass of water, hold your nose, and knock it straight back."

"Okay, here goes." She shut her eyes, and drank it all in one go.

"How was it?"

"Not as bad as I expected." She released her nose, and opened her eyes. "It won't make me sick, will it?"

"No, you'll be fine. There won't be any after-effects. What time are you due at Ghost Placements?"

"They said to be at their offices by one pm."

"You'd better get a move on, then. I'll give it a few hours, and then track you in the human world."

"What if the powder doesn't work? I don't want to be stuck there."

"Relax, Blodwyn. There's absolutely nothing to worry about." I hoped I sounded more confident than I actually felt.

***

After I'd left Blodwyn, I magicked myself back to Washbridge where I was due to have lunch with my darling sister, and my long-lost friend, Lolly Jolly.

Chess was a few doors down from Bar Piranha. Kathy was waiting for me outside.

"You conned me," I said.

"That's no way to thank me for buying you lunch."

"You'd already agreed to meet Lolly, and thought that dragging me along would take some of the pressure off you."

"That's a very cynical view."

"Cynical, but deadly accurate. I know you like the back of my hand."

"Exactly how well do you know the back of your hand?"

"What?"

"Are you really that familiar with the back of your hand?"

"It's just a saying, Kathy."

"I know that, but now you know what it's like to be on the other side of this kind of madness."

"I have no idea what you're talking about."

"You're always analysing common sayings."

"Rubbish. I don't do that."

"Don't you remember that week-long rant you had about something being the best thing since sliced bread?"

Before I could refute Kathy's unsubstantiated accusation, Lolly appeared. What on earth was she wearing? I'd never seen so many lollipops. They were on her dress, her bag, her shoes and even on the ribbon in her hair.

"Lovely to see you both." She hugged Kathy and then me. "What's this place like? Are there any male strippers?"

"It's Chess, as in the board game. Not chest as in—err—chest."

"That's disappointing." Lolly frowned. "Still, we'll be able to chat more easily without any distractions."

Yay! For being able to chat to Lolly.

The place was much more sophisticated than I'd expected: Stylish décor, attentive staff, and classical music. We were seated at a table that was smack bang in the centre of the restaurant.

Halfway through the main course, Lolly put down her knife and fork.

"Do you two remember that song we used to sing?"

"No," I lied.

Kathy shook her head, but I could tell by her expression that she did.

"You must remember it. We always used to sing it whenever we were together. Now, how did it go?"

"I'm not sure this is the place for—"

"*Lolly, Lolly is always jolly.*"

I glanced around the room. All eyes were on us. I wanted the floor to open up and swallow me.

"*Not Polly, not Molly. Lolly, Lolly. Never sad. Always Jolly.*"

The waiter was glaring at us.

"Those were the days, weren't they, girls?" Lolly was oblivious to the attention she was attracting.

Thankfully, we managed to get through the rest of the meal without a repeat performance of the Lolly Jolly song.

"I guess we should be making a move," I said.

"Yeah, I have to get back to the shop." Kathy stood up.

"This has been great!" Lolly beamed. "But there's one more thing we have to do."

I didn't like the sound of that.

"Don't you remember how much we loved this stuff when we were kids?" She took a small can out of her bag, and before Kathy or I could react, she'd sprayed us both with 'silly string'.

Lolly was in hysterics. Kathy looked as mortified as I felt.

"Ladies, I'm sorry." The waiter was stern faced. "This kind of behaviour cannot be tolerated in Chess."

"Lighten up, misery chops," Lolly said.

"We were just leaving." I stood up.

Everyone in the restaurant was staring at us, and tutting.

When we got to the desk, Lolly began to root around inside her handbag. "I'm so sorry, girls. I'm such a pudding brain. I've come out without my purse."

Chapter 20

After Lolly had left us, Kathy reminded me that this was the same trick she'd played on us when we were kids.

"Don't you remember, Jill?" We'd all go down to the shop for sweets, and when we got there, Lolly would say she'd lost her money."

"Oh yeah. It's all coming back to me."

"I've never been so embarrassed as when she started singing." Kathy cringed. "Did you see all the looks we got?"

"It's a wonder we didn't get shown the door there and then."

"I'm done with her. The next time she calls, I'll say I'm busy."

"Me too. I'd better get going."

"I'll see you tomorrow."

"Tomorrow?"

"Don't tell me you've forgotten. It's the 'We' concert."

"Oh, right, yeah. I'll be counting the minutes."

I waited until Kathy had left, and then cast the spell that would allow me to lock onto Blodwyn. The signal was strong, which meant she wasn't too far away. After finding a quiet back alley, I magicked myself towards the signal, but just far enough away so that I didn't land smack bang in the middle of their operation. I didn't want to scare them away before I knew what they were doing with those hapless souls.

Souls? Get it? Come on — get with the program.

I landed on an area of wasteland. Not far from where I was standing was a building which had once been a factory, but was now close to derelict. Blodwyn's signal was coming from somewhere inside. Fortunately, all the windows in the building had been boarded up, so I didn't need to use the 'invisible' spell to hide my approach. I'd no sooner reached the building than the gates opened, and a white van came speeding out. The signal, which until then had been static, was now moving away from me. She was obviously inside the van, so I cast the 'faster' spell to allow me to keep up with it. I also cast the 'invisible' spell because I didn't want to attract any unwanted attention, as I raced along the road at speeds of up to fifty miles per hour.

The van eventually came to a halt on the village green in West Chipping, where a travelling funfair was being set up. It wasn't the same one I'd been to in Washbridge, but the rides were very similar. The van came to a halt near to the ghost train. I positioned myself next to the back doors of the van. When the wizard who had been driving it opened the door, several ghosts, who were all visible to me, climbed out. Blodwyn, who had a haunted look on her face, was at the back of the line. As soon as she jumped down from the van, I took hold of her arm. She almost jumped out of her skin because I was still invisible.

"It's okay," I whispered. "It's me. Hang on."

I magicked us both back to Washbridge city centre where I reversed the 'invisible' spell.

"Are you okay, Blodwyn?"

"I don't know. I think so."

"What happened?"

"They were taking us to the ghost train. They were going to force us to work there."

"That explains a lot."

"What do you mean?"

"I went to a funfair in Washbridge with my sister, Kathy, and her kids. Kathy said the ghosts in the ghost train ride were the most realistic she'd ever seen. There's little wonder—they're obviously real ghosts. What I don't understand, though, is how come you and all the other ghosts are visible to humans. Don't you have to attach yourself to be seen?"

"Normally, yes, but they've developed some kind of weird formula, which they injected us with. It makes us visible to humans, and also stops us going back to Ghost Town."

"That's terrible."

"We have to do something to help the others. There must be hundreds of them around the country."

Blodwyn was right. All the ghosts who had disappeared must have been sold to funfairs. I had to find a way to liberate them, and get them back to Ghost Town.

"Don't worry," I reassured her. "I'll find a way to rescue them, but first we'd better get you back to GT."

"How? The injection they gave me won't allow me to go back. Not for twenty-four hours, at least."

"Is that how long it lasts?"

"Yes. They said we'd have to be injected every day."

"Okay. In that case, we need to find a place for you to stay overnight. Tomorrow, when the formula has worn off, we can get you back. I'm afraid I can't take you home with me—Jack would ask too many questions. You'll have to stay in my office overnight. Will that be okay?"

"Sure."

"There's a sofa in there, but you may have to fight the cat for it."

***

Jules was in the office by herself.

"Has Lules gone?"

"Yeah. She went to meet her boyfriend, Dilbert."

"Right. Jules, this is Blodwyn."

"Hi." Jules managed a smile, but I could tell she was somewhat shocked by Blodwyn's appearance.

"Go through to my office, Blodwyn. I'll be with you in a minute."

"Is she okay?" Jules asked, when Blodwyn had left us. "She looks terribly pale."

"She's fine. She's just had a bit of a shock."

"Is she a new client?"

"Client? Yes. That's who she is."

"Shall I make her a drink?"

"No—err—we've just had one. Look, it's quiet, why don't you shoot off home."

"Already? Are you sure?"

"Yes, off you go."

"Thanks. Gilbert and I are meeting Lules and Dilbert later, so it will give me more time to get ready."

"Great. Enjoy your evening."

Blodwyn was already fast asleep on the sofa.

"Who does she think she is?" Winky had a disgruntled look on his face. "Coming in here, and throwing me off the sofa?"

"She's had a rough day."

"Don't talk to me about rough days. I got a splinter in my paw this morning. It was this long." He held his paws apart.

"Six inches? Do you think you might be exaggerating a tad?"

"It was at least that long. I was still recuperating when she appeared, and stole my sofa. What's up with her anyway? She looks like she's just seen a ghost."

"She *is* a ghost. Don't ask; it's a long story."

"How about some salmon to compensate me for the loss of the sofa? And to help me forget about the ordeal of the splinter."

"Okay then, but only a small helping."

Blodwyn slept for the best part of two hours, but then sat up with a start.

"Are you okay?" I asked.

"Yeah, but I'll be glad when I can get back to GT."

"I'll have to leave soon because we're going to a dinner and dance tonight. Would you like me to order you some food first?"

"I wouldn't say no to a pizza."

"Me neither," Winky chipped in.

I waited until the pizza had been delivered, and then left Blodwyn with the promise that I'd contact my father to let him know that she was safe, and that she would be back home the following day.

***

Before I went home, I decided to check in on the twins. It was the first day of the new drive-thru, and I wanted to see how things were going.

"You got here just in time." Pearl greeted me. "We're just about to officially open the drive-thru."

"Oh? I thought you would have opened first thing this morning."

"We had planned to, but the stepladder thing wasn't going to work, so we brought in a joiner to create a small platform for us to stand on. Come and take a look."

She led the way into the back, where Amber was standing on the wooden platform.

"That looks much better." I nodded my approval.

"It is." Amber demonstrated by tapping on the hatch window.

"How exactly are you going to manage the drive-thru?" I asked. "Have you employed more staff to help?"

"There's no need." Pearl picked up two headsets from the table, and handed one to Amber. "We can serve in the shop, and take orders from the drive-thru using these."

"Ready?" Amber asked.

Pearl gave her sister the thumbs up, and Amber opened the hatch. The drive-thru was officially open.

It was something of an anti-climax because there were no customers in the new drive-thru yet, but the twins still seemed upbeat.

"The orders will soon start to flow once word gets around," Pearl said, as we made our way back to the front of the shop.

I had to admit that the twins certainly looked very high-tech in their headsets.

Pearl was halfway through serving a wizard at the counter when her headset crackled into life. I was very impressed — it had taken less than a minute for their first drive-thru customer to arrive.

Or had it?

"Can I get a taxi at the north side of the market place?"

the crackling voice said.

"Please get off this frequency," Pearl said into the mic.

The headsets crackled into life again.

"What can I get you?" Amber answered this time.

"Billy? Can you make a pick-up outside the swimming baths?"

The girls exchanged a worried look.

"What's going on?" I said. "That sounded like a taxi company."

"Just teething problems," Amber reassured me.

"Hello? Can I get a taxi outside the town hall, please?"

Oh dear. It was time to leave them to it.

***

Jack had spent the last hour getting ready.

"You look lovely." He gave me a peck on the lips.

"Thanks."

"And?" He looked at me, expectantly.

"And what?"

"How do I look?"

"Very smart. You scrub up well."

"Did you remember to practise your bossa nova steps, today?"

"Every opportunity I got."

Jack was determined that we put on a good performance. Me? I was just hoping that there would be plenty of wine to get me through the evening.

***

"Good evening, Jack." A plump man with a red nose

greeted us at the door. "And this must be the beautiful Jill. I've heard a lot about you, young lady."

"This is Sergeant Russell," Jack said, by way of introduction.

"You can call me Bobby, Jill."

Bobby the bobby? Seriously? "Nice to meet you, Bobby."

"I've put you on table twenty-three, next to the cloakroom."

Jack took my hand and we started across the dance floor.

"Ouch!" I stumbled.

"Jill?" Jack managed to catch me before I hit the floor. "Are you okay?"

"I've twisted my ankle." That would teach me to wear such stupidly high heels.

"Can you walk?"

"Just about, but you'll have to support me."

We'd only gone a few more steps when Jack stopped dead in his tracks.

"What's wrong?"

"That's all I need."

"What's the matter?" I still had no idea what was bothering him.

"Look who we're sharing a table with." He pointed.

"No. Please tell me this is a joke."

"I wish it was."

Leo Riley was seated at the table next to the cloakroom.

"Who's the woman with him?" I said.

"That's his wife."

"He's married?" I was surprised because I'd thought he was having a fling with medical examiner, Sheila Treetop.

It seemed he was an even bigger slime ball than I'd thought he was.

"Hello, Leo." Jack feigned politeness.

"Jack? Jill?" Leo was obviously as delighted to see us as we were to see him.

"Aren't you going to introduce us, Leo?" The woman seated next to Riley nudged him.

"Sorry. This is Jack Maxwell. He used to work at Washbridge Station, and is at West Chipping now. And this is Jill Gooder."

"Nice to meet you both." The woman smiled. "I'm Miley Riley."

I tried—honestly, I did. But *Miley Riley*? How could I not laugh?

Jack and Leo both glared at me.

"Sorry. I was just thinking about something Jack said in the car, on the way over here. He's such a comedian."

Miley Riley turned out to be a delightful person. Why she was with a cheating scumbag like Leo was beyond me.

The food was surprisingly good for a dinner and dance. I opted for the turkey; the other three had beef. When the meal was over, a five-piece band took to the stage. As the dance floor began to fill, Jack asked if I was okay to dance.

"Sorry. My ankle still feels very weak."

"I'll dance with you, Jack." Miley stood up. "Leo can't dance for that stick up his backside."

Leo Riley was not amused.

"Having fun, Leo?" I asked, once Jack and Miley were on the dancefloor.

He ignored me.

"Miley seems to be enjoying herself."

He continued to ignore me.

"Isn't Tops here, tonight?"

"Don't you dare mention her name in front of Miley. There's nothing going on between me and Sheila Treetop."

"So why don't you want your wife to know about her?"

"Shut it!"

"I'm beginning to think you don't like me, Leo. Or do I still have to call you Detective Riley when we're socialising?"

"We're not socialising. I'll be polite for Miley's sake, but don't push it."

"How is the Lee Sparks case going?"

"I'm not discussing an ongoing investigation with you."

"Investigation? What investigation? From what I hear, you decided Kylie Jay was the murderer from the get-go, despite having the flimsiest of evidence."

"I've told you. I'm not discussing it."

"You've got the wrong person behind bars."

"Says you. This one isn't rocket science. He actually called the murderer by name live on air, and her fingerprints are all over the murder weapon."

"It should be obvious to anyone with half a brain that the only reason Kylie's fingerprints are on the knife is because she grabbed the handle, purely as a reflex action."

Although Kylie had denied touching the knife, it was the only explanation that made any sense. My theory was that the shock had caused her to blank it out.

"Do you think we're completely stupid? Don't you think we thought of that? The problem with that excuse is that the knife came from Kylie Jay's flat."

What? I hadn't seen that coming.

Chapter 21

"You're quiet," Jack said, over breakfast.

I shrugged.

"What's wrong?"

"Nothing. I'm absolutely fine."

"Okay."

"If you must know, I didn't appreciate being dumped with Leo Riley all evening."

"It wasn't all evening."

"Most of it."

"Sorry, but Miley is a really good dancer. Her foxtrot is a sight to behold."

"My ankle is fine. Just in case you were wondering."

"I only didn't mention it because you seemed to be walking okay when we came home last night."

"It could have deteriorated overnight."

"Did it?"

"I'll survive."

"Did you and Leo make a connection?"

"The only connection I want to make with that man is with my hands tight around his neck. I used to think that you were a pain in the butt, but you've got nothing on that idiot. He did let something slip, though."

"Oh? What was that?"

"I'm working on the Lee Sparks case. His girlfriend has been charged with his murder. Her mother is my client."

"Did the info from Riley help your client?"

"Not really. It actually makes things look worse for her. Even so, I'd rather know than be in the dark."

"Am I forgiven for last night?"

"Give me a kiss, and I'll think about it."

***

Constance Bowler had agreed to see me at short notice. This time, we met in her office at GT police headquarters.

"I like your offices," I said. "They're much more modern than those in either the human or sup world."

"Thanks. They've only recently been renovated.

"I wanted to see you because I now know what the ghost traffickers are up to."

"That was quick."

"I had someone sign up with Ghost Placements, and then I tracked them when they were taken to the human world. That end of the operation is being run by wizards. They've developed some kind of formula which makes the ghosts visible to any human. It also prevents the ghosts from returning to GT for twenty-four hours. They have to be given an injection every day."

"That's terrible."

"You haven't heard the worst of it yet. They're selling the ghosts to funfairs where they're being used in ghost train rides."

"What happened to your colleague?"

"I was able to snatch her back. I've left her in my office in Washbridge overnight until the formula wears off. I'm going to check on her later. She should be able to go back to GT by then."

"We have to close this operation down, and we have to do it now."

"I've been thinking about that. Trying to find all the ghosts who have been sold into ghost train slavery would be a fool's errand, because there are any number of funfairs up and down the country. I suggest we shut down the central operation where they produce the formula. If we can turn off the supply, the ghosts will all be able to return to GT of their own volition after twenty-four hours."

"Is that something you can do?"

"I'll need some help from the rogue retrievers, but that shouldn't be a problem."

"Great. I'll make sure we close down the Ghost Placements office at this end."

***

Back in Washbridge, I made a call to Daze.

"I'm actually on a few days leave, Jill. I'm in the middle of moving into my apartment, but if you want to come over and update me, I'll be able to get Blaze on it for you."

"Okay. It didn't take you long to find somewhere."

"I haven't—not really. My boss insisted that I move to Washbridge by the end of the month. I checked out a few places, but they weren't suitable. Haze said I could move in with her until I find somewhere permanent. I'm in what used to be the old sock factory. Do you know it?"

"Yeah. I can be there in a few minutes."

"I'm on the top floor. Apartment five-zero-three."

***

I parked around the back of the apartment block. From the outside, the building didn't look that much different to when it had been the sock factory.

"Pretty? Pretty? Where are you?" A male voice called.

I almost ran straight into a giant of a werewolf who came charging out of the apartment block.

"I'm sorry," he apologised. "You haven't seen a cat around here, have you?"

"No."

"Okay, thanks. Pretty? Where are you?"

What kind of name is 'Pretty' for a cat?

What? There's nothing wrong with 'Winky'.

The lift was out of order, so I was forced to trudge up the stairs. By the time I reached apartment five-zero-three, I was out of breath. I really did need to make better use of my free life-time membership at I-Sweat.

"Are you okay, Jill? You look terrible."

"I'll be alright in a minute." I took a few deep breaths. "The lift isn't working."

"Tell me about it. I had to carry all my stuff up here."

And yet, something told me she probably hadn't even broken sweat.

"I like the apartment. It's huge. Did you say Haze lives here alone?"

"Yeah."

"Why don't you move in permanently? It's not like there isn't enough room. How many bedrooms are there?"

"There are two. Haze is doing me a favour by letting me stay here until I find somewhere else, but I know she wouldn't want it to be permanent. She likes her own space, and to be honest, so do I. I don't plan on sharing unless it turns out to be the only option."

"I'm sorry to trouble you with this while you're in the middle of moving in."

"That's okay. It sounded kind of urgent."

"Yeah, it is."

"Blaze should be here at any minute. He was going to help me unpack, but it might be better if I put him on your case."

"Won't it slow you down if you don't have his help?"

"Quite the reverse." She grinned. "I'll get things done much quicker without him under my feet, and besides, he'll enjoy the responsibility."

Just then, there was a knock at the door.

"That will be him. Will you let him in, please?"

"Jill?" Blaze looked surprised to see me. "I didn't realise that you were helping out too."

"She isn't." Daze pulled open a large cardboard box. "Jill needs our assistance, but I'm pretty much tied up. I told her that you'd help her."

"Me?" Blaze's face lit up. "Great! What's up?"

I brought Blaze up to speed on the ghost trafficking problem. Although Daze continued to unpack, it was obvious that she was listening to us.

"What's your plan?" Daze asked when I'd finished the story.

"I thought I was meant to be taking charge of this?" Blaze said.

"Sorry. You are." She went back to her unpacking.

"What's your plan, Jill?" Blaze said.

"It would be impossible to get around every funfair in the country, to release the ghosts individually. If we can cut off the source of the formula that is preventing them from returning to Ghost Town, then they should be able to make their own way back within twenty-four hours."

"Where is the formula being made?" Blaze took out a small notepad.

"According to my contact, it's being produced in the

small factory that they use as a holding area for the ghosts when they're first brought through to the human world. I can give you the address."

Blaze scribbled it down. "Okay. I think I have everything I need. I'll get a few more rogue retrievers over here, and we'll hit the factory later this afternoon."

"Do you want me to come with you?" I asked.

"No need. I'll let you know when it's done." He slipped the notepad into his pocket, and made for the door.

"Be careful!" Daze called after him.

"Will he be okay?" I asked Daze, after Blaze had left.

"He'll be fine. I know I give him a hard time, but he's come on in leaps and bounds. He'll soon be able to work solo."

"Have you told *him* that?"

"Of course I haven't." She grinned.

"On my way up here, I almost ran into one of your neighbours. Literally. A giant of a werewolf. He was looking for a cat."

"That would be Charlie. I haven't had a chance to meet many of the neighbours yet, but I did run into Charlie on my first day. He gave me a hand carrying some of my stuff upstairs. He's a real sweetheart."

"Didn't Haze say that she hadn't found the neighbours to be particularly welcoming?"

"Yes, but to be honest, that's only to be expected. I can't imagine any sup would be overjoyed to find they have a rogue retriever as a new neighbour."

***

If Daze was prepared to trust Blaze, then I'd have to. I'd seriously considered insisting that I go with him, but I didn't want to undermine his confidence. I'd just have to be patient (not one of my better qualities—just in case you were wondering).

Back at my office building, I bumped into Brent on the stairs.

"I hope you're making the most of your free lifetime membership, Jill."

"Of course. One or two sessions every day."

"Did you realise that the computer system tracks who has been in the gym?" He grinned.

"Okay, I haven't been in for a few days. You know how it is. Busy, busy, busy."

"If you hear some banging today, don't be alarmed. We're just having CCTV cameras set up inside the gym."

"Oh? Have those bad guys been back?"

"No. You seem to have scared them away. We're still having a few problems overnight, though. A few things are still being moved, and every morning we find lots of animal fur on the equipment. We have to get to the bottom of it."

"Right. Well, good luck."

"And don't be a stranger. There's a treadmill with your name on it."

"Don't worry. I'll be there."

Mrs V was seated at the desk closest to the door.

"All alone today, Mrs V?"

"Yes, thank goodness."

"I thought you and Jules were getting along okay now?"

"We are. I can handle Jules. It's that sister of hers who's getting on my nerves."

"Lules?"

"What kind of stupid name is that?"

"Did she say something to upset you?"

"She's obviously keen to get out of that dreadful black pudding factory. It's clear she has ambitions to follow in her sister's footsteps."

"I thought she wanted to be a model?"

"Apparently she wants to be a model *and* a PA."

"Does she have any qualifications?"

"No, but then *someone*, mentioning no names, gave her sister a job even though she had no qualifications."

Touché.

"Lules kept asking me if I'd thought about retiring completely, and if the stairs were too much for me."

"Oh dear." I couldn't help but smile.

"It isn't funny, Jill. It's like having a vulture hovering overhead."

"You have nothing to worry about, Mrs V. I've told you before. There will be a place for you here as long as you want it."

"Thank you, dear. I guess I already knew that, but it's still reassuring to hear."

When I walked into my office, there was no sign of Blodwyn.

Once again, as soon as Winky saw me, he stuffed a piece of paper into the lining on the underside of the sofa. Just how stupid did he think I was? It was painfully obvious that he'd wanted me to see him do it.

"Morning, Winky."

"Morning. Just in case you thought I was hiding something, I wasn't."

"That's good."

"I wouldn't blame you if you were suspicious."

"I'm not. Not in the least."

"Good. I wouldn't want there to be any mistrust between us."

"It's fine. I trust you completely."

"You do? That's good."

"Do you know what happened to the woman who stayed here overnight?"

"She disappeared. Literally. One minute she was lying on *my* sofa, and the next, 'puff', she'd gone. I can't say I was sorry to see the back of her because she snored like a trooper."

The formula must have worn off, and allowed Blodwyn to return to GT.

"By the way, Winky, I bumped into Brent from I-Sweat just now. They're still convinced that there's something going on in the gym overnight. They're having CCTV cameras installed today, so you'd better wind down your illegal gym scam, and quickly."

"There's no need. I'm not worried."

"They're going to see everything. How do you expect to continue?"

"I have a contingency plan for such an eventuality, of course."

"What kind of contingency plan?"

"That would be telling."

Chapter 22

I had an hour or so to kill before I was due to meet with Kylie's flatmate. After the excitement of the morning, I was ready for a rest, so I planned to kick off my shoes, sit back at my desk and recharge my batteries.

"Mirabel! You can't go in there!"

Grandma came charging into my office, closely pursued by an exasperated Mrs V.

"I don't need your permission to see my granddaughter, Annabel."

"It's okay, Mrs V, thanks. I'll handle this."

Mrs V chuntered something, but then left us to it. Needless to say, Winky had already exited, stage right.

"What can I do for you, Grandma?"

"I'm through to the audition stage."

"You are?"

"Why are you so surprised? I'm obviously ideal for the part."

"Yes, sorry, it's just that there must have been a lot of applicants."

"It's down to a shortlist of ten. The screen test is on Saturday."

"Congratulations on getting this far, and good luck on Saturday."

"*Good luck*? It's no good relying on *good luck*. No one ever got anywhere by relying on *good luck*. Do you know what the magic word is?"

"Abracadabra?"

"No. It's *preparation*."

I was close.

"And that's why I'm here." She produced two sheets of

paper from her bag, and handed one to me.

"What's this?"

"My shopping list. What do you think it is? I want you to help me to practise my lines. You'll be Lavinia."

"Who's Lavinia?"

"She's my daughter. I'm Esmeralda, the head of the Crawshaw family."

"Crawshaw?"

"I didn't pick the names! Are you going to help or are you just going to stand there asking stupid questions all day?"

"I am kind of busy."

"When I walked through the door just now, you were arranging your paperclips by size."

"It saves time later."

"Are you ready to start?"

"I have an appointment in an hour."

"We'd better get on with it, then. Yours is the first line."

"Okay, here goes. I'll never be as powerful a witch as you, Ma."

"Is that the best you can do? How am I supposed to bring out my best performance if you aren't even trying?"

"Sorry. I'll have another go." I switched to full-on thesp mode. "I'll never be as powerful a witch as you, Ma."

"One day you might, Lavinia, but only if you believe in the power of magic."

There weren't words to describe how bad her performance was.

"What do you think?" Grandma said. "Not bad, eh?"

She was right. It wasn't bad. It was terrible. Winky would have been more believable in the part.

"Not bad for a first attempt." I lied. "It might be better

though if you were just yourself."

"Myself? Don't you understand anything about acting? I have to inhabit the being that is Esmeralda."

"Right, okay. Sorry."

We spent the next hour reading through the lines. On a scale of nought to wooden, Grandma was a definite two-by-four. The ironic thing was that if she'd read the lines as herself, she would have been ideal for the part, but there was no telling her.

"Break a leg, then," I said, as she was about to leave.

"What a horrible thing to say. And to your own flesh and blood, too."

"No! I didn't—err—mean—err—it's just what they say in the theatre. Never mind. Good luck on Saturday."

"She doesn't stand a chance." Winky reappeared. "I've seen dead mice with more acting ability than her."

Harsh, but true.

***

Sandra Johnson, Kylie's flatmate, was wearing PJs when she answered the door.

"Sorry about these." She gestured to her attire. "I only got up an hour ago. Heavy night."

"No problem. Thanks for seeing me."

"Do you mind if I do the ironing while we talk? I'm completely out of tops."

"Carry on." I had to move a pile of magazines so I could sit on the only chair in the kitchen. "Have you and Kylie been flatmates for long?"

"A couple of years. We were at school together. When

I'd had enough of living with my parents, I asked Kylie if she fancied sharing."

"Do you two get on okay?"

"Mostly, yeah, but she doesn't like it when I borrow her clothes and stuff. And, she's always telling me that I'm untidy."

She had a point.

"How well did you know Lee Sparks?"

"I know you're not supposed to say bad things about the dead, but he was a complete tool."

"What in particular didn't you like about him?"

"He was so full of himself. He thought he was better than everyone else. But the worst thing was the way he treated Kylie."

"What do you mean?"

"I wouldn't let any guy talk to me the way that he talked to her."

"Was he ever physically abusive towards her?"

"Not that I saw, but I wouldn't have put it past him."

"How was she on the morning of the day that Lee was murdered?"

"In a terrible state. They'd had a big bust-up the night before."

"What about?"

Sandra shrugged. "I'm not sure, but it was the worst I'd seen Kylie. Her mother was here too."

"Did she often come over?"

"Not particularly. Kylie hated her mum sticking her nose in. She'd come over to try to talk Kylie into dumping Lee."

"Was she going to?"

"I don't think so. She and her mum had a real shouting

match, and then her mum stormed out."

"I understand the police have been to see you?"

"Yeah. They pretty much asked the same questions as you have."

"And they showed you the knife?"

She nodded. "It was definitely one of ours."

"Had you noticed it was missing?"

"No. I had no idea. Not until the police came by."

***

Kathy, Peter and Jack were all waiting for me downstairs.

This week was going from bad to worse. The previous day, I'd had to put up with laughing boy, Leo Riley, at the dinner and dance. Now, I had the 'We' concert to deal with. Unless of course I could wheedle my way out of it.

"Jill!" Jack called. "Are you ready?"

"I don't think I'm going to make it."

He came charging upstairs.

"Why not? What's wrong?"

"It's my ankle." I hobbled across the room. "It seems to have taken a turn for the worse. The three of you had better go without me."

"You're coming. Hurry up or we'll be late."

"What about my ankle?" I hobbled a little more. "I'll never make it."

"There's nothing wrong with your ankle."

"How can you say that? You don't know how painful it is."

"I know there's nothing wrong with it because you're limping on the wrong foot." He set off back downstairs.

Oh bum!

"Are you excited?" Kathy greeted me when I eventually joined them.

"Thrilled to bits. I don't understand why we have to go so early. The main act won't start for ages."

"We want to see the support act," Jack said.

"Even so. It's only a ten-minute drive to Washbridge Arena."

"It's not at the Arena. It's at Chipping Stadium."

"Really? I didn't realise that 'We' could fill that place."

"She could have filled it twice over. Come on or we'll miss the start."

Chipping Stadium was halfway between Washbridge and West Chipping. It was more modern and much larger than the fleapit that was Washbridge Arena. Kathy, Peter and Jack spent a month's salary on a program, and three scarves with 'We In Concert' on them. They offered to get one for me, but I preferred to retain some semblance of dignity.

I was relieved to find that the standing area was practically empty. I'd been worried it might be overcrowded and claustrophobic.

"Do you need the loo, Jill?" Jack asked, as we waited for the support act to come on stage.

"I'm okay."

"Are you sure? It'll get busy later."

I glanced around—there were no more than a dozen people in the standing area. "I'm fine."

While the others were at the loo, I tried to work out how much the takings were likely to be for a show like this. It was an awful lot of money, which made it all the more depressing that I'd declined the chance to join The Coven when they were relatively unknown.

Kathy, Peter and Jack got back just as the support act came on stage. The Fangs were a four-piece heavy metal band. They were dressed as vampires, and looked pretty authentic. That was hardly surprising given that they were real vampires.

They don't look as good as we did at the cosplay," Jack shouted over their music.

"What cosplay?" Kathy looked puzzled. "You never mentioned that to me."

"I've been trying to forget about it."

"Jill and I went as vampires." Jack took out his phone. "Look, I have photos."

"You look great, Jack," Kathy said. "Why didn't you have fangs, Jill?"

"I did, but they made my jaw ache, so I took them out for a while."

"It looks like fun. Pete and I should go with you next time."

Never going to happen.

"That's a great idea." Jack was way too enthusiastic. "I'll check with Tony and Clare when the next one is."

"Who are Tony and Clare?"

"Our new neighbours. Hasn't Jill told you about them?"

"Jill never tells me anything."

The standing area was now much more crowded; I could barely move.

"I need the loo!" I shouted to Jack.

"I asked you earlier."

"I didn't need it then."

"Good luck. The nearest one is over in that corner."

It took me forever to fight my way through a million smelly armpits, but I eventually made it. When I came out of the loo, who should I bump into but Betty Longbottom. Standing next to her was a tall young man who looked like a cross between a vampire and a punk rocker.

"Hi, Jill," Betty said. "I didn't realise you were a Fangs fan."

"Me? No, I just got dragged here by Jack. He's a massive 'We' fan."

"This is Sid."

"Nice to meet you, Sid."

Sid grunted something, and then wiped his nose on the sleeve of his jumper. Betty certainly knew how to pick them.

"I'm going to the bogs," Sid announced, and then headed into the loo.

"Are you a Fangs fan, Betty?"

"Not really. I'm only here because Sid is obsessed with them."

"How did you two meet?"

"He came into the shop, looking for some crab earrings."

"I suppose I'd better fight my way back to Jack."

"Are you in the mosh pit?"

"Unfortunately, yes. Bye, Betty."

By the time I eventually made it back to Jack and the others, The Fangs had just finished their set.

"I was beginning to think you'd gone home," Jack said. "Are you okay?"

"Yeah. I bumped into Betty Longbottom. She has a new boyfriend."

I might as well have been talking to myself because at that precise moment, 'We', AKA Brenda, walked on stage, and the whole stadium erupted.

I have to be honest, Brenda put on an excellent show, but by the time she came to the end of her set, I was exhausted. There was so little room in the mosh pit that I could barely move — my legs were beginning to cramp.

"Come on." I pulled at Jack's sleeve. "Let's get going."

"Wait. She'll be back for an encore."

I glanced at the stage which was now in darkness. "No, she won't. She's done." I desperately wanted to get out of there, but the crowd behind me weren't budging, so I figured if I could just get up onto the stage, I could make my way to the side much quicker.

"Jill! What are you doing?" Jack called after me, but I was in no mood to listen. I just wanted to get out of there.

At that precise moment, the stage lights came back on, and the music started up. A huge cheer rose from the crowd as Brenda walked onto the stage. Out of the corner of my eye, I saw a giant of a man rushing towards me.

"Get off the stage!" the security man yelled. He obviously thought I was trying to get to the star. "Get down!"

I turned around, but before I could climb off the stage, he pushed me. Fortunately, the crowd cushioned my fall, and the next thing I knew, I was crowd surfing around the mosh pit.

Twenty minutes later, the three of us were on our way back to the car park.

"I never had you down as a crowd surfer, Jill," Kathy

said, and the three of them broke down in fits of laughter.

Chapter 23

It was the next morning, and I was desperate to forget the crowd surfing debacle of the previous evening. In my experience, I'd always found the best way to 'forget' was to eat chocolate.

"Jack, where's that bar of chocolate that was in the cupboard?"

"I ate it yesterday."

"Great. I suppose I'll have to call in at the corner shop, then."

"Ask Jack Corner if my bowling magazine has come in, will you?"

"Okay."

Jack Corner was standing on his box behind the counter.

"Good morning, young lady. Can I introduce you to my new assistant?"

I glanced around but could see no one.

"Missy. Say hello."

The young woman climbed up onto her own box, next to him. "Nice to meet you. I'm Melissa Muffet, but everyone calls me Missy."

Missy Muffet? Someone was having a laugh.

"Nice to meet you, Missy. I'm Jill."

"What can I get for you today, Jill?"

"Just this bar of chocolate, please."

"Trying to forget something?"

"Yeah. How did you guess?"

"Chocolate works for me too."

"How is the VHS library going, Jack?" I thought I should ask.

"We've got off to a quiet start, but I'm still very confident. I'm a great believer in investing in the future."

"Right, well, I'd better get going."

"Not without the thought for the day."

"Go on then."

"It's always darkest just before the eggs hatch."

Another classic.

I was half way back to the house when I realised that I'd forgotten to ask about Jack's magazine. I could have turned around and gone back to the shop.

I could have, but I didn't.

What? I was doing him a favour. No one should ever have to read a bowling magazine.

***

Jules was by herself in the office.

"No Mrs V today?"

"She'll be in later. She had an appointment at her chiropodist for—"

"It's okay. I don't need to know the gory details."

"Did you say you were going to the 'We' concert, Jill?"

"Yeah." I sighed. "We went last night."

"Did you see that idiot in the mosh pit?"

"Sorry?"

"Look." She held up her phone. "Someone put up this video on YouTube. Some old girl decided to crowd surf during the encore. What an idiot."

Old girl? Fortunately, when I'd fallen off the stage, I'd landed face-down on the crowd, so at least no one could tell from the video that it was me.

"Were you in the mosh pit, Jill?"

"Me? No, we were in the seated area."

"That's what I like about you. You act your age. I hate to see older people making fools of themselves."

"How much do you think we'll find?" Winky was on the phone, and apparently hadn't heard me come through the door. "Really? As much as that? Are you sure? Okay, but we mustn't let anyone else know about it. We don't want a thousand other treasure hunters to get there before us." Just then, he glanced around and saw me standing in the doorway. "No. I don't need any double-glazing, thank you very much. And don't call me again. Bye."

What a performance!

"What was all that about, Winky?"

"That? Oh, nothing. Just some double-glazing salesman."

"I thought I heard you mention hidden treasure?"

"Oh—err—yes. The company was called Hidden Treasure Double Glazing."

He was such a terrible liar. What was he up to?

***

I'd promised to visit Kylie in prison later, to bring her up to date on my investigation. Things weren't looking very good for her so far. Although several people obviously had it in for Lee Sparks, I hadn't found any evidence which might link them to the crime.

First, I wanted to check how Cuppy C's new drive-thru was working out. Hopefully, the twins would have resolved the teething problems with the headsets.

When I arrived, neither of the girls was wearing one.

"Where are your headsets? Are you still having problems with the taxis?"

"No. We got that sorted out," Pearl said.

"So how come no one is serving at the drive-thru hatch?"

"There was another slight problem." Amber sighed.

"What kind of problem?"

"A pickup truck pulled into the drive-thru. It was too wide for the alleyway, and it kind of got stuck."

I laughed but immediately regretted it. "Sorry. How did they get it out?"

"They haven't yet. They reckon they'll have to dismantle the truck and take it out in bits."

"That's rather unfortunate. How long will the drive-thru be closed?"

"It's closed permanently," Pearl said.

"How come?"

"Apparently, we were supposed to tell the council about our plans." Amber sounded indignant. "How were we meant to know that?"

"Didn't you apply for planning permission before going ahead with this?"

They both shook their heads.

"You'll just have to keep it closed until you get the permission."

"We won't get it. The council have already been in contact to say that they won't allow us to have the drive-thru because the alleyway isn't wide enough."

"What will you do about the hatch?"

"Use it to throw out people who annoy us."

Why were they both looking at me?

"Jill! Over here!" Aunt Lucy called to me from a corner table.

"I didn't see you there. Are you by yourself?"

"I've been shopping with Mavis Redbottle, but she had to go to the hospital to visit her mum. Won't you join me?"

"Just for a few minutes."

"How come you haven't got anything to eat or drink, Jill?"

"I think I've upset the twins."

"Oh?"

"I made the mistake of asking about the drive-thru."

"Oh dear." She laughed. "I don't know how they keep coming up with these crazy ideas." She turned to the counter. "Amber! Bring Jill her usual, would you?"

"Thanks, Aunt Lucy."

"It's the least I can do. I owe you for helping me out with the dress for the dinner and dance."

"I didn't do anything. That was down to Monica."

"I know, but if it hadn't been for you, I would never have contacted her."

"How was the dance?"

"I really enjoyed it. I'd been expecting the worst, but it turns out that grim reapers really know how to have a good time. I suppose if you do that for a living, you need to be able to let your hair down."

"Does that mean you don't mind Lester doing the job now?"

"I'd still rather he did something else, but I don't feel as bad about it as I did."

"There you are!" Amber slammed down the drink and

muffin, and then went back to the counter.

"I don't think she's forgiven me yet."

"Don't look now, but there's someone headed this way." Aunt Lucy gestured towards the door.

Why do people say: *'Don't look now'*? It always results in the exact opposite reaction.

"Miles?"

"I thought I saw you in here!" His face was so red it looked as though it would explode at any moment.

"Is there a problem?"

"Is there a problem?" He mocked. "What do you think?"

"I'm guessing 'yes', but I have no idea what."

"Why did you get Mindy to dump me?"

"I did no such thing."

"You were the one who found out she'd been sabotaging the muffins."

"She told you it was her?"

"Yes. Just before she said she never wanted to see me again."

"That's hardly my fault. Don't you think it might have more to do with the fact that you were cheating on her with Flora and/or Laura?"

"That's none of your business."

"No, but it's certainly Mindy's business, and if she has dumped you, I can't say I blame her. You had it coming."

"You'll regret this."

"Have you forgotten our agreement? I was to find out who was sabotaging your cakes, and you were to halt all vendettas against me and my family."

"You can forget that!"

"You're going back on your word?"

"That agreement ended the moment you turned Mindy

against me." He started towards the door. "You'll rue the day."

"Nice talking to you, too, Miles. Don't be a stranger."

***

I magicked myself back to Washbridge, to pick up the car. It was a thirty-minute drive to the prison where Kylie was being held, and I wasn't looking forward to telling her the bad news.

I'd just parked in the prison car park when my phone rang. It was a very excited Blaze.

"Mission accomplished, Jill."

"That's great. Any problems?"

"Not really. The wizards are all behind bars back in Candlefield. There were a couple of ghosts in the factory, waiting to be sent out to a funfair. They'd already been injected with the formula so we couldn't send them straight back to GT."

"Where are they now?"

"Daze said they could stay with her overnight until the formula wears off."

"Thanks, Blaze. Sounds like a job well done."

"My pleasure, Jill. It was nice to get the chance to run a mission for a change."

Kylie's hopeful expression made what I was about to say even harder.

"I'm afraid that so far I haven't managed to come up with anything that is going to help you."

It was as though someone had knocked all the air out of her. She sank forward in her chair, and began to sob.

"I didn't do it. I didn't kill Lee. I can't stay in here. I'll never survive."

"You mustn't give up hope. I'm going to carry on with the investigation."

"I'm done for."

She wept for several minutes. Nothing I could have said at that point would have helped, so I allowed her to get it out of her system.

***

Jenny Black, one of the cleaners at Radio Wash had given me the phone number of her boss, a Mrs Draycott. I wanted to find out from her if anyone else had the combination to the rear door lock.

I called the number, and it rang out for quite a while. I was just about to give up when someone answered.

"Hello?" The female voice was barely audible.

"Is that Mrs Draycott?"

"Who's this?"

"Jenny Black gave me your number. My name is Jill Gooder. I'm investigating the murder of Lee Sparks."

"This isn't a good time. I haven't been well."

"I'm really sorry to trouble you just now, but I wondered if you'd answer a couple of quick questions."

"Are you the police?"

"No. I'm a private investigator."

"Who are you working for?"

"Doris Jay. Kylie's—"

"I know Doris."

"Oh? I just wanted to ask if you knew of anyone else who would have access to the rear door of the radio station? Apart from you and the other cleaners?"

"Only the security men, but Doris would already know that."

"How would she know?"

"Doris used to work at the station. In fact, she was my boss until she decided to retire. I took her job; Susie took mine."

"Doris Jay was on the cleaning staff at the radio station?"

"Until about six months ago, yes. How is Doris holding up?"

"She's doing okay under the circumstances."

"Are you sure? The last time I bumped into her, a couple of months back, she was still beating herself up for getting Kylie into this mess."

"How do you mean?"

"Didn't you know? Doris was the one who introduced Kylie to Sparks. It was not long after Sparks started here, and before we all knew what he was really like. Kylie would often drop into the station to see her mum."

"Right. Just one last question: Has the combination for the rear door been changed since Doris left her job?"

"It hasn't been changed in years, as far as I'm aware."

"I see. Thank you for your help. I hope you feel better soon."

Suddenly, everything began to make sense.

Chapter 24

I'd arranged to meet with Doris Jay at her house.

"Come in, Jill. I hope you have some good news for me. Kylie is beginning to despair."

"I know. I went to see her this morning."

"You did?"

"I promised that I'd keep her posted on my investigation."

"Of course. Were you able to put her mind at ease? Have you identified any other suspects?"

"Just one."

"I suppose that's better than nothing. Have you informed the police of your findings?"

"I'm hoping that you'll do that for me."

"I don't follow."

"You clearly love your daughter, Doris. That's why I don't understand how you could allow her to spend so long locked up like this."

"I still don't know what you mean."

"I think you do. You used to work at Radio Wash as a cleaner, didn't you?"

"Err—yes, but that's a while ago now."

"And it was you who originally introduced Kylie to Lee Sparks."

The colour drained from her face. "Do you mind if I sit down?"

"Please do. You blamed yourself for the predicament that Kylie found herself in, didn't you?"

"Of course I did. It was just after Sparks joined the station. He seemed okay at first. Kylie often used to come and see me at work. I was cleaning his studio before his show was due to go on air. Kylie was with me when Sparks walked in. She was thrilled to meet him, but I never thought anything would come of it."

"But it did."

"He asked her for her phone number. I didn't even know he'd done it. The next thing I knew, they were an item. If I could go back in time, I would never have let him get anywhere near my little baby."

"Did she tell you how he mistreated her?"

"She didn't need to. I saw the change in her, and I knew what had caused it."

"Why were you at Kylie's apartment on the morning of the murder?"

"She'd phoned me the night before, in hysterics. I went around there to make sure that she was okay, and to tell her to dump him once and for all."

"But she wouldn't?"

"She was still besotted with him. It was like he had some kind of power over her."

"So you decided to do something about it yourself. That's why you took the knife from Kylie's flat."

"I only intended to warn him off, but he just laughed. The next thing I knew, he was bleeding. I don't even remember doing it."

"Didn't it occur to you that Kylie's prints might already be on the knife?"

"I never even thought about it. I wasn't thinking straight."

"Why didn't they find your prints on there too?"

"I was wearing gloves that morning because it was cold."

"What I really don't understand is why you would let

Kylie take the fall."

"I thought once the police realised that Kylie wasn't the murderer, they'd release her. That's why I came to you. I knew there were plenty of other people who hated Sparks. I thought if you could come up with some other possible suspects, it might convince the police to let Kylie go."

"You know what you have to do now, don't you?"

She nodded. "I'll go to the police station, and hand myself in, but would you mind doing me a favour, Jill?"

"If I can."

"Tell Kylie I'm sorry for putting her through all of this."

I didn't feel it was necessary to accompany Doris Jay to the police station because there was no doubt in my mind that she would make a full confession. I still couldn't understand why Doris hadn't come forward as soon as her daughter was arrested. She may have been afraid, and hoped that the police or I would uncover other suspects, but that was irrelevant. She should have confessed there and then. Even the short length of time that Kylie had spent behind bars could have damaged her irreparably. And how was Kylie going to feel when she discovered that her mother was the murderer, and that she had failed to come forward immediately?

And, who was going to pay my bill now? Doris Jay would be behind bars for a very long time—quite possibly the rest of her life. That was not going to help my year-end figures.

***

Mrs V was back at her desk.

"How's the foot, Mrs V?"

"Much better. My new chiropodist is an absolute whizz with corns. I'll let you have his number."

"I don't have corns."

"Not now, maybe, but at your age, it's only a matter of time."

At my age?

She scribbled his number on a scrap of paper, and handed it to me. Jules was enjoying this way too much for my liking.

Winky was on his phone again, and far too engrossed to notice me. "Yeah. We have to do it on Tuesday. Once we've got it, we'll be rich." He ended the call, then turned around, and noticed I was standing there. "How much of that did you hear?"

"Nothing. I just walked in the door."

"Are you sure?"

"Positive. Why? What's so top secret?"

"Nothing. Nothing at all."

I'd barely had time to sit down at my desk when Grandma appeared. Mrs V and Jules hadn't even tried to stop her—they'd obviously realised it would be a waste of time.

"Aren't you supposed to be at the screen test this afternoon?" I said.

"Aren't *we*, don't you mean? And yes, we are."

"Hold on. I never said I'd go with you."

"You didn't need to. I did."

"I happen to be busy."

"Very amusing. Come on! Grab your bag."

"I'm not sure the studio will allow you to bring someone with you."

"That's where you're wrong. They make a point of saying we can bring one friend or relative along if we want to."

Drat!

"Are we going to magic ourselves there?"

"No, I thought you could drive. I can practise my lines in the car en-route."

It was a fifty-mile trip to Swing Slide Studios, but it felt more like a thousand. Grandma's audition piece comprised of no more than a dozen lines, but she must have read them out loud at least a million times.

No exaggeration.

On each read-thru, she tried to vary her performance in some way, but they all had one thing in common. They were all wooden.

"What do you think, Jill?" she asked, after attempt number six-thousand and seventy-two.

"Very good."

"Do you prefer that one to the one before?"

"Do *you*?"

"Yes, I think I do."

"Me too. That one was definitely better."

Once Grandma and I had signed in at reception, we were escorted to a small set where the director, Jordan Warewithall, greeted everyone, "Welcome one and all. I'm very excited to meet you, and very much looking forward to seeing your screen tests. At the end of today, we'll choose one of you to take the part of Esmeralda. The important thing is that you try to relax and enjoy yourself."

"Stuff and nonsense," Grandma said, under her breath. "The important thing is that I get the part."

"You can only do your best," I whispered. "You mustn't be too disappointed if you don't get it."

"What kind of loser attitude is that? Just look at this crowd. Not one of them would make a good witch."

Grandma and I were the only sups present. It was certainly true that she was the only one there who actually looked the part, but would that be enough? Having heard her practising her lines, I seriously doubted it.

The director continued, "You'll be called one-by-one, first to make-up, and then to your screen test. Any questions?"

Only one person raised a hand, and there are no prizes for guessing who that was.

"How much does this pay?"

"The full details of the contract will be ironed out with the successful candidate."

"Will this part get star billing?"

"We won't think about screen credits until much later." The director looked around. "Anyone else have a question? No? In that case, I'll see each of you later, in front of the camera."

Moments later, the first woman was called through to make-up. After another thirty minutes, a second woman was called. When the first woman returned from her screen test, everyone swarmed around her, to ask how it went—everyone except Grandma.

"Don't you want to know how she went on?"

"Why would I care? This is all just a formality."

"Mirabel Millbright!" The make-up woman called.

"Shall I wait here?" I asked.

"No. Come with me. I want you to see this, so you can report back to everyone on my success."

Oh boy!

The make-up woman looked rather harassed. "Do I call you Mirabel?"

"Mrs Millbright will do fine."

"I see you applied your own make-up before you came. I'm afraid that wart will have to go. It's a nice attempt, but it isn't very realistic."

"Could I have a quick word?" I grabbed the woman's arm, and dragged her to the other side of the room.

"What is it? I'm really pushed for time."

"The wart on her nose is real," I said, in a hushed voice.

She laughed. "That's very funny."

"I'm being serious. It's real. If you cut it off, there'll be blood everywhere."

"Oh, my goodness." She sounded horrified. "Thank you for warning me."

She walked back over to Grandma, who looked all set to rip the poor woman's head off.

"Just a little blusher, then," the make-up woman said. "There, that's fine. Off you go, through that door over there."

"What did you say to that stupid woman?" Grandma demanded.

"I—err—asked if she was having trouble with her eyesight. She seemed to be squinting. Apparently, she left her glasses at home this morning."

"Sheer incompetence. How do I look?"

"You look great."

"Mirabel Millbright!" The director beckoned for us to

join him. "This is Lucy Potts, she plays the part of your daughter."

"Pleased to meet you, Mirabel." Lucy smiled.

"You're a bit old for the part, aren't you, dear?" Grandma looked her up and down.

"Err—right—if everyone is ready." The director had one of his minions lead Grandma and Lucy onto the set. I stayed behind the cameras.

Once everyone was in position, the director called, "Action!"

If you try to imagine how bad it was, and then multiply it by one hundred, you still wouldn't be close. It wasn't just that Grandma kept forgetting her lines; she also insisted on berating her fellow actor and even the director, at every opportunity.

"Right! That's a wrap!" the director shouted.

"I think we need one more take," Grandma suggested. "I could add a little more passion to that final line."

"No need. That last take was—err—perfect. Thank you, Mirabel."

"When do we get to talk about the contract?" Grandma asked.

"Those discussions will take place later, after we've finished all of the auditions."

"I could tell the others to go home now, if you like?" Grandma offered. "That would save us all some time."

"Err—no—thanks. After they've travelled all this way, I think it's only fair they get their turn in front of the camera."

"How much longer is all of this going to take?" Grandma complained to me, an hour later.

"There are still another four to audition."

"I need some fresh air."

"I don't think you're meant to leave the set."

But it was too late. Grandma was already on her way back to reception.

Great!

Two hours later, and the last woman had just gone through for her screen test, but there was still no sign of Grandma. Where was she? Had she got lost?

I traced my way back to the studio entrance, and asked the woman on reception if she had seen Grandma.

"Does she have a really big wart on her nose?"

"Yes, that's her."

"She went out a while ago."

"Did you see which way she went?"

"She turned left out of the door."

"Thanks."

As soon as I got out onto the street, I could hear singing. Or at least, what passed for singing where Grandma was concerned. Fifty yards up the road from the studio was a pub called The Pickled Trout. In the bar, singing at the top of her voice, was my very own pickled trout.

"Grandma! What are you playing at?"

"Can you get her out of here?" the plump man behind the bar said. "She's scaring away the other customers."

"Sorry. I'll see to it. Come on, Grandma."

"Jilly, Jill, Jill." She hiccupped. "Where's the contract? Is it time to sign?"

"They're about to announce the successful candidate. Come on, we need to get back."

I somehow managed to guide her back to the studio just

as the director returned to address us all.

"Thank you all once again for coming in today. I've seen so many wonderful performances, it's a pity that there can only be one winner. It gives me great pleasure to announce—"

"Thank you." Grandma suddenly stepped forward. "I am very honoured—"

I managed to pull her back.

"As I was saying," the director continued. "It gives me great pleasure to announce that the part of Esmeralda goes to Anne Craymouse."

Anne stepped forward, in floods of tears. Everyone else rushed to congratulate her. Everyone except Grandma.

"This is an outrage!" Grandma yelled. "That woman is no witch. I'll show you what a real witch can do."

I wasn't sure which spell she was about to cast, and I didn't want to hang around to find out, so I grabbed her by the arm and led her away.

"What do you think you're doing?" Grandma fought me every step of the way back to the car. "Let me go. I'll show him what a real witch can do."

"Get in the car, Grandma."

Once I'd got her in, I fastened her seat belt, jumped into the driver's seat, and sped away. Fortunately, within a few minutes, she was fast asleep.

The good news was that I didn't have to listen to her reciting her lines on the way back. The bad news was that I had to listen to her snoring instead.

The perfect end to a perfect day.

Chapter 25

We'd had a great weekend. On Saturday, Jack and I had taken a drive out into the countryside, and grabbed lunch at a lovely little pub situated at the top of a picturesque valley. On Sunday morning, Jack had pottered about in the garden while I supervised, and then I made Sunday lunch.

See! I can be domesticated when I put my mind to it.

By Monday morning, my batteries were well and truly recharged, and I felt ready for whatever the week might throw at me.

When I stepped into my office, Winky was on the phone again.

"Tomorrow, yeah. Don't worry. No one else knows." He glanced around, and spotted me. "Can't talk now— someone has just come in. Okay, bye."

"Morning, Winky."

"Morning."

"What's with all the mysterious phone calls?"

He shrugged. "I don't know what you're talking about."

Hmm? Maybe there really was something going on that he didn't want anyone to know about.

"I have Kylie Jay to see you," Mrs V was walking with a bit of a limp.

"Are you okay, Mrs V?"

"My corns are playing up again. Is it okay if I pop out to the chiropodist later?"

"Of course. Would you send Kylie in, please?"

Kylie Jay looked happier than the last time I'd seen her,

but not much.

"I just wanted to come by and thank you for getting me out of prison. I'm not sure I could have taken much more."

"How are you doing?"

"Okay, but I'm very worried about Mum."

"Have you seen her?"

"Only for a few minutes. I still can't believe she killed Lee. I blame myself. I should have dumped him ages ago, like Mum said. If I had, none of this would have happened. Lee would still be alive, and Mum would be free. What do you think will happen to her?"

"It doesn't look good. She's confessed to the murder, so it's just a question of how long a sentence they hand down."

"Is there anything I can do to help her?"

"You should get a chance to speak up for her before sentencing. I wasn't sure you'd want to after she failed to come forward."

"I don't hold that against her—she was just scared. Mum hoped your investigation might uncover other suspects, and that would be enough to get me released. How did you work out that she'd done it?"

"It was a number of things. She had the motive because the man was hurting her child. She'd been at your flat that morning, so had access to the murder weapon. Your mum had the combination to the lock on the rear door at Radio Wash, so was able to gain access without being captured on CCTV. Everyone who heard Lee's last words assumed he was addressing you when he said, 'Jay'. But that wasn't true because he used to call you 'Little Jay'. Jenny Black told me that he always called the cleaners by their surnames, so when he said 'Jay', he was actually speaking to your mother."

"The worst part about all of this is that I was going there to finish with him."

"But didn't you tell your mother you wouldn't do that?"

"I hated it when Mum tried to run my life, so when she said I should finish with Lee, I instinctively told her to butt out and mind her own business. That's why she took matters into her own hands. If I'd told her the truth—that I was going to dump him, she would probably have gone home."

"You mustn't blame yourself for any of this."

"That's easier said than done." Kylie stood up. "By the way, you must let me have your bill."

"That isn't your responsibility. You weren't my client."

"Mum told me to ask for it. The payment will come out of her account."

"Okay. If you're sure."

After Kylie had left, I reflected on the case. I'd found the murderer, and got an innocent person released from prison. And yet, I took no pleasure from it at all.

***

I was still thinking about Kylie and Doris Jay when Kathy rang.

"Whatever is wrong with your grandmother today?"

"How would I know? I haven't seen her since Friday. Why? What's she up to?"

"I wish I knew. She's been grumbling to herself all morning. Something about an audition being fixed? And missing the chance for Hollywood stardom?"

"Has she been at the cocktails?"

"I don't think so."

"Is that why you called?"

"No. I wanted to remind you about taking Lizzie to Washbridge House. Are you still up for that?"

"Yeah. I just need to sort out a date with Mad."

"Okay. Talking of ghosts, Mikey went to the funfair again on Saturday."

"I'm surprised he managed to talk you into going back there."

"He didn't. Lizzie and I went shopping. One of Mikey's friends from school was going to the funfair, and the boy's parents said Mikey could go with them."

"Did he have fun?"

"I think so, but the thing he was most looking forward to, turned out to be a bit of a damp squib. The main reason he wanted to go back there was to have another ride on the ghost train. Mikey reckons there were hardly any ghosts in there this time, and those that were there, weren't very realistic."

***

I was finding it hard to concentrate on my paperclip sorting because Winky was snoring so loudly. I'd shouted at him a few times, but he simply rolled over and started again. I was just about to nudge him when I remembered the slip of paper that I'd seen him hide in the lining of the sofa. What harm could it do to take a look?

It appeared to be some kind of hand-drawn map of Washbridge city centre. A dotted line had been marked along the roads, and where that line terminated was a big cross with the word 'treasure' written underneath it.

I checked to see if Winky had stirred, but he was still fast asleep. If I'd had any sense, I would have put the note back, and forgotten all about it. But as we all know, common sense is not my strong suit, so I decided to check it out. Obviously, I didn't actually believe there was any treasure—I'm not totally stupid—I just needed to stretch my legs.

What do you mean the self-delusion continues?

With treasure map in hand, I sneaked out of my office—being careful not to wake Winky.

"I'm going out for a while, Jules. If anyone asks where I am, you don't know."

"But I don't know."

"Even better."

Although I knew I would ultimately be disappointed, it was all rather exciting. It reminded me of the treasure hunts that my adoptive parents had sometimes organised for me and Kathy, in the school holidays. She always seemed to win—knowing her, she'd probably cheated.

I was getting close. According to the map, the treasure should be just around the next corner. This was an area of Washbridge that I rarely visited, so I had no idea what to expect.

"What the—?"

Just then my phone rang.

"Congratulations!" Winky said. "You have found the treasure."

I couldn't speak; I was too busy staring, open-mouthed,

at the shop in front of me. The one with the huge banner that read: 'Grand Opening Today', draped above the door.

The shop was called 'The Salmon Emporium'.

"Are you still there?" Winky's voice brought me back down to earth.

"You set me up."

"Of course I did, but you have to admit this was a cool plan. Anyway, while you're there, I believe they're running an opening offer on red. You might as well get stocked up."

"I understand how you tricked me into taking the map, but how did you know the precise moment when I arrived here?"

"That would be the tracking device in your phone."

Once again, that cat had done me up like a kipper.

***

That evening, Jack called to say he'd be home late, so I treated myself to a delicious pizza from the guys at One Minute. I'd just finished eating it when there was a knock at the door.

"Ms Nightowl?"

Desdemona Nightowl was headmistress of Candlefield Academy of Supernatural Studies, or CASS for short.

"I'm sorry to turn up unannounced like this."

"That's okay. Do come in."

"Are you alone?"

"Yes. Jack has to work late. Won't you come through to the lounge?"

"Thank you."

In addition to her freaky walking stick, she was carrying

a small rectangular parcel wrapped in plain, brown paper.

"Can I get you a drink?"

"Nothing for me, thank you. I can't stay long."

"How is Tommy?"

"None the worse for his ordeal. It's in connection with that incident that I'm here today."

"Oh?"

"It's school policy to ensure that all passageways are adequately lit; there is less chance of accidents that way. After your visit, I asked the maintenance department to install lights in the passageway that you uncovered. In the course of doing so, they found this." She placed the parcel onto the coffee table.

"What is it?"

"Please, open it."

I tore off the brown paper to reveal a small framed portrait of a woman.

"Who is it?"

"I was hoping you might know."

"Me? I don't have a clue. Why did you bring it to me?"

"Turn it over."

I did as she said. There was something written on the back. It read: *second or third, matters not. This portrait shall belong to whoever discovers the passageway in which it was hidden.*

"What does that mean? *Second* or *third?*" I asked.

"I have no idea."

"I don't think I should have this. The school should keep it."

"No. It belongs to you now. Think of it as a token of our gratitude for saving Tommy Bestwick."

"Okay. Thank you."

Just then, the door opened, and Jack walked in.

"Are there any burgers in the freezer, Jill? Oh? Sorry. I didn't realise you had company."

"I was just leaving." Ms Nightowl smiled at Jack, but didn't introduce herself.

I walked her to the door where we spoke in hushed voices.

"Thanks for coming over."

"My pleasure. You really must visit us again. You still owe us a talk."

"I'd love to."

"I'll be in touch, then."

When I got back to the lounge, Jack was studying the painting.

"Who was that strange old bird?"

"She owns the bric-a-brac shop in town. The one near to the post office."

"Why was she here?"

"I bought this painting today. She insisted on cleaning the frame before I took it away. I was going to collect it tomorrow, but she was passing so she decided to deliver it."

"Since when were you interested in paintings?"

"I'm not, but I spotted this, and thought it was pretty."

"It looks expensive."

"It wasn't. It's only a print."

"Who is that in the picture?"

"I don't know."

"Where are you going to hang it?"

I didn't answer. I was too stunned by what I'd just noticed.

"Jill?"

"Err—I don't know. I'm not sure if I still like it." I picked it up. "I think I'll stick it in the back bedroom for now." I hurried upstairs before Jack spotted it too.

The woman in the portrait had a pendant around her neck. A pendant with the initials 'JB' engraved on it.

ALSO BY ADELE ABBOTT

The Witch P.I. Mysteries:

Witch Is When... (Books #1 to #12)
Witch Is When It All Began
Witch Is When Life Got Complicated
Witch Is When Everything Went Crazy
Witch Is When Things Fell Apart
Witch Is When The Bubble Burst
Witch Is When The Penny Dropped
Witch Is When The Floodgates Opened
Witch Is When The Hammer Fell
Witch Is When My Heart Broke
Witch Is When I Said Goodbye
Witch Is When Stuff Got Serious
Witch Is When All Was Revealed

Witch Is Why... (Books #13 to #24)
Witch Is Why Time Stood Still
Witch is Why The Laughter Stopped
Witch is Why Another Door Opened
Witch is Why Two Became One
Witch is Why The Moon Disappeared
Witch is Why The Wolf Howled
Witch is Why The Music Stopped
Witch is Why A Pin Dropped
Witch is Why The Owl Returned
Witch is Why The Search Began
Witch is Why Promises Were Broken
Witch is Why It Was Over

Witch Is How... (Books #25 to #36)
Witch is How Things Had Changed
Witch is How Poison Tasted Good
Witch is How The Mirror Lied
Witch is How The Tables Turned
Witch is How The Drought Ended
Witch is How The Dice Fell
Witch is How The Biscuits Disappeared
Witch is How Dreams Became Reality
Witch is How Bells Were Saved
Witch is How To Fool Cats
Witch is How To Lose Big
Witch is How Life Changed Forever

The Susan Hall Mysteries:
Whoops! Our New Flatmate Is A Human.
Whoops! All The Money Went Missing.

AUTHOR'S WEB SITE
http:www.AdeleAbbott.com

FACEBOOK
http://www.facebook.com/AdeleAbbottAuthor

MAILING LIST
(new release notifications only)
http:/AdeleAbbott.com/adele/new-releases/

Made in the USA
Middletown, DE
08 September 2017